By Janet Evanovich

Motor Mouth • *Metro Girl*

Hero at Large • *The Grand Finale* • *Foul Play*
Naughty Neighbor • *Wife for Hire*
Thanksgiving • *Smitten* • *Manhunt*
Back to the Bedroom • *Love Overboard*
The Rocky Road to Romance

One for the Money • *Two for the Dough*
Three to Get Deadly • *Four to Score* • *High Five*
Hot Six • *Seven Up* • *Hard Eight*
Visions of Sugar Plums • *To the Nines*
Ten Big Ones • *Eleven on Top*
Twelve Sharp • *Plum Lovin'*
Lean Mean Thirteen • *Plum Lucky*
Fearless Fourteen • *Plum Spooky*
Finger Lickin' Fifteen

The timbre of his voice lowered. "Someone who takes better care of your . . . mechanical needs?"

Chris rolled her eyes. She was late for work, her car had just succumbed to terminal neglect, and her feet were freezing. She was in no mood to field a double entendre from a scruffy stranger . . . even if he did make her heart skip a few beats. She stood abruptly, hitting her head on the inside of the hood. There was a loud *spronnng*, and Chris jumped away just in time to see the hood come crashing down on two long, sweatshirt-clad arms.

His breath hissed from between clenched teeth. He swore softly, resting his forehead on the cool metal of the car. "Nice work, lady," he rasped. "Do you always cripple men who stop to help you? Or am I special?"

Chris opened her eyes wide in horror. "I'm sorry—it was an accident!"

"Uh-huh."

Chris glared at him. "Well, you shouldn't be making passes at women you stop to help. It's like Sir Walter Raleigh carrying some grateful lady over a mud puddle and then trying to sneak a look under her skirt when he sets her down. This was a well-deserved accident. An act of God," she tagged on for dramatic effect.

He nodded his head in mute agreement. Beads of sweat had begun to appear at his hairline. "Do you suppose God would mind if you got the damn hood off my arms?"

JANET EVANOVICH

Hero at Large

(Originally published under the name Steffie Hall)

HARPER

An Imprint of HarperCollinsPublishers

HARPER

An Imprint of HarperCollins*Publishers*
10 East 53rd Street
New York, New York 10022-5299

First Harper paperback printing: April 2010

HarperCollins® and Harper® are registered trademarks of Harper-Collins Publishers.

Printed in the United States of America

Visit Harper paperbacks on the World Wide Web at
www.harpercollins.com

10 9 8 7 6 5 4 3 2 1

Chapter 1

Chris Nelson muttered an indiscernible oath and expelled a cloud of frost into the bone-chilling early-morning air. Even in the inky predawn blackness, it was clear that a new splotch of oil had mysteriously grown beneath her battered tan hatchback during the night. She plunged her key into the lock and wrenched the dented, rusting door open, then slid behind the wheel and tried the ignition. Nothing.

"Just start one more time, and tomorrow I'll get you fixed," she pledged, knowing full well that it was an empty promise. She didn't believe in getting cars fixed—she felt too hopelessly intimidated by car mechanics. As a world-class athlete she'd conducted media interviews with the aplomb of a seasoned celebrity. She'd displayed good-humored optimism as a runner-up and honest satisfaction as a winner, and earned a worldwide reputation for her feisty personality and quick wit under pressure. But she knew in her heart of hearts that while she could hold her own with the president of the United States, she would never be a match for a man holding an air wrench. She cringed at the memory of her last experience, when she'd paid an exorbitant amount to fix a glamus—while meekly suspecting that no such part existed.

No, she decided, keeping her thoughts silent— and thus secret from the car—it was much more sensible simply to drive the dying machine into the ground, walk away from it with whatever dignity she could muster, and buy a new one. She gingerly tried the ignition one more time and almost cheered out loud when it caught. She pulled away from her Fairfax, Virginia, town house with a glorious feeling of victory, closing her eyes to the red light flashing on the dashboard. Dismissing the clouds of gray smoke as condensation, she bravely eased the sputtering car onto the highway.

Ten minutes later when she stopped for a red light on the Little River Turnpike, the car shuddered, belched an acrid blast of opaque exhaust, and stalled out. Chris felt her heart drop to her stomach. "Please," she whispered, wrapping her fingers gently around the steering wheel, "tell me you're not ready for the big junkyard in the sky."

She narrowed her eyes and patted the dashboard. "I'll let you rest a minute, and then we'll try it again." The light changed. Traffic rushed past in the November gloom: Northern Virginia was en route to the Pentagon and downtown D.C. Chris held her breath and tried again. Nothing.

"Dammit." She peered into her rearview mirror at headlights waiting patiently behind her. Throwing her hands up in frustration, she punched the button that turned on the emergency flashers. The lights shining into her back window were high. Probably a truck. That was good—men who drove trucks always knew a lot about car engines, she reasoned. She watched hopefully as the driver emerged and strode toward her, then shifted her gaze to the flashing red light she'd so easily ignored only minutes ago.

Knuckles rapped on Chris' side window. "Got a problem?"

Chris' eyes stayed glued to the warning light on her dash. "It just suddenly stopped. I think it might have something to do with this little red light."

"Why don't you try to kick it over one more time."

She turned the key and listened morosely to the churning motor.

"Stop."

"Only thing in decent working order on this whole crummy car is the stupid warning light," Chris muttered through gritted teeth. Her peripheral vision registered a shift of weight, and she felt rather than saw the grin of good-humored masculine resignation.

"Maybe we should push it over to the shoulder, and I'll take a look under the hood."

Several minutes later, Chris stomped her feet in the cold as she watched him poke around at the engine. He was very tall—maybe six-two, she guessed—and nicely put together. He wore scuffed, waffle-soled construction worker's boots and well-washed jeans that clung suggestively to long, muscular legs. A faded navy blue hooded sweatshirt draped comfortably over broad shoulders. A smudged tan down vest hung unbuttoned over the sweat shirt.

He flicked a flashlight beam over rubber tubing and fan belt, his black hair falling in unkempt waves over his eyes. A heavy beard made his dark skin look villainously swarthy, and the tousled hair curled over his ears and halfway down his neck. He made an attempt to brush it back onto his forehead and noticed Chris watching him. "I need a haircut," he explained, flashing a boyish grin that displayed perfect white teeth.

Chris felt her heart tumble unexpectedly at his disarming smile and immediately an image of Little Red Riding Hood and the big bad wolf popped into her head. What a ridiculous thing to think of—yet there was definitely a predatory air about him. Wolfish, in an attractive sort of way, she decided. And incredibly handsome . . . but a slob. Probably on his way to pour a foundation or dig a septic system.

Determined to prove herself invulnerable to his charms, she leaned on the front quarter panel and stuck her head under the hood with him. "Well?" she asked expectantly, "what do you think?"

"For starters . . . there's not a drop of oil in it."

Chris looked up and found herself staring into magnetic blue-black eyes made even more compelling by thick curling lashes and crinkly smile lines that testified to an active, outdoor life and a generous sense of humor. She watched dry-mouthed as he directed his flashlight to the riot of yellow-orange curls that surrounded her perfectly oval face. His inspection traveled from her almond-shaped hazel eyes, down to her small pixie nose and her bow-shaped mouth that shone with just a touch of pink lip gloss. She licked her lips and answered in a voice that suddenly sounded strangely husky, "Is that bad?"

The look of incredulity that fluttered across his eyes was replaced immediately with a gently mocking curiosity. He played the light over her ringless hands. "I think you need a new man in your life." The timbre of his voice lowered. "Someone who takes better care of your . . . mechanical needs?"

Chris rolled her eyes. She was late for work, her car had just succumbed to terminal neglect, and her feet were freezing. She was in no mood to field a double entendre from a scruffy stranger . . . even if he did make her heart skip a few beats. She stood abruptly, hitting her head on the inside of the hood. There was a loud *spronnng*, and Chris jumped away just in time to see the hood come crashing down on two long, sweatshirt–clad arms.

His breath hissed from between clenched teeth. He swore softly, resting his forehead on the cool metal of the car. "Nice work, lady," he rasped. "Do you always cripple men who stop to help you? Or am I special?"

Chris opened her eyes wide in horror. "I'm sorry—it was an accident!"

"Uh-huh."

Chris glared at him. "Well, you shouldn't be making passes at women you stop to help. It's like Sir Walter Raleigh carrying some grateful lady over a mud puddle and then trying to sneak a look under her skirt when he sets her down. This was a well-deserved accident. An act of God," she tagged on for dramatic effect.

He nodded his head in mute agreement. Beads of sweat had begun to appear at his hairline. "Do you suppose God would mind if you got the damn hood off my arms?"

"Sorry." She held the hood while he awkwardly started to move his arms. He flexed one gingerly, then winced when he tried to raise the other. Chris Nelson was the sort of person who rescued baby birds and felt guilty about stepping on ants. She cried when people were hurt on television, and sent money to aid starving children, but she found it difficult to muster any sympathy for the man standing in front of her. He was so big and capable looking, and so aggressive. He was so roguishly shabby. And he silently emanated a casually checked sexuality that she suspected could knock her socks off if she gave it half a chance.

Standing to his full, imposing height, he cradled

his left arm tenderly against his body. "My right arm seems to be okay, but the left is definitely broken." His voice was quiet, calm. "Is there a hospital near here?"

"There are two hospitals in the area—both about ten minutes away. Maybe a little longer in morning traffic."

He looked at her expectantly. "Well?"

"Well, what?"

"Lady, you just broke my arm. Aren't you at least going to offer to drive me to the hospital?"

Chris looked at him tentatively, her lip caught between her teeth, while she debated the danger of being alone in a car with him.

"For Pete's sake, I'm not going to attack you. I've got a broken arm."

"You look disreputable."

His gaze drifted down over himself in amazement. "I suppose you're right." He tipped his head back and laughed softly. "I've been called lots of things, but you're the first person in a long time to tell me I'm disreputable looking." He motioned to his truck. "I hate to be pushy, but my arm is killing me, and I can't both drive and shift my truck with only one arm. Since you're the cause of this disaster, I think the least you can do is drive me to a doctor."

He was right, she thought dismally. "Okay. I'll take you to the hospital." She shook her finger at him in warning. "So help me . . . if you make one false move I'll drive you straight to the state police."

His gaze swept slowly over her, and Chris felt suddenly unaccountably flustered—self-conscious of her tousled curls, her slim, athletic body bundled in her gray running suit and bright red vest. "You're not a minor, are you?"

Chris pulled a large athletic bag from the back seat of her car and locked it. "I'm twenty-nine, and if you tell me I look like Little Orphan Annie I might break your other arm."

"There is a resemblance."

"Don't push it." She stood facing his truck. It was a single cab Toyota Tacoma, dark gray with large wheels—and it seemed to be in perfect condition. Sure, it's easy for him, she thought grimly. He probably knows if it has a glamus. A huge black dog sat behind the wheel. Chris looked at the man beside her. "There's a dog in there."

"Yeah."

"That's the second-biggest dog I've ever seen."

"It's a Rottweiler."

"It must weigh two hundred pounds. We won't all fit."

"Of course we will. This truck seats three."

"This truck would have to have rubber doors to seat three."

He swung himself into the truck and settled beside the panting Rottweiler. "Come on," he coaxed. "He's a good dog. See? He's smiling. He likes you."

Chris set her bag on the floor between his feet and trudged around to the driver's side. "Why me?" she groaned. "Why do these things always happen to me?" She opened the driver's side door and slid in next to the mountain of dog, trying politely to nudge him over. He didn't move. He draped his huge head on her shoulder and drooled down the front of her red vest. Chris rolled her eyes in disgust. "Oh for goodness' sake. Hey, you!" she called between the dog's ears. "What's your name?"

There was a brief hesitation. "Ken Callahan."

"Ken Callahan, I can't drive with your dog drooling on me."

He sighed. "Okay."

The passenger door opened and slammed shut. Chris watched Ken Callahan jog around the truck. Not her type, she told herself, but she had to admire his style. Even with a broken arm, he moved with the fluid ease of an athlete. He opened the door and jerked his thumb at Chris in an obvious order. "Out!" Maneuvering his large frame behind the wheel, he used his good arm to shove the dog clear to the window. He settled himself next to the Rottweiler and straddled the gearshift. "Is this better?"

"Do you drool?"

"Another ten minutes with you, and I'm going to be drooling and babbling and committing mayhem."

Chris slid behind the wheel again and found herself pressed thigh to thigh with Ken Callahan. There wasn't an inch to spare between the dog and the man. And the gearshift was hopelessly lost from sight between Ken Callahan's legs. *I should have left well enough alone*—she grimaced—*I was better off with the Rottweiler.*

"Um . . . Ken?"—she tried to shift in her seat—"We don't all fit in this truck."

"If I'd known you were going to break my arm, I would have left my dog at home." His voice was rapidly losing its calm modulation.

Wriggling again, Chris shot him a black look. "Don't get cranky. For two cents I'd leave you stranded here."

"I'd give you the two cents, but I can't get into my pocket with my broken arm."

Chris narrowed her eyes and counted to ten. "Can't he ride in back?"

"He'll jump out—and please don't suggest that *I* ride in back . . . it's starting to rain."

Chris squinted miserably at the windshield. He was right. It was raining. "Fine," she said through clenched teeth, "just keep out of my way." Ken Callahan made a fruitless attempt to move his long legs while she turned the key in the ignition. She switched the lights on, but the interior was barely lit by the glowing dashboard. Pressing her lips tightly together, she reached between his legs in search of the gearshift.

There was a sharp intake of breath, and the man squirmed beside her. "Lady, if you'll just tell me what it is you're looking for . . . I'll be glad to help you find it."

She swallowed and willed her voice not to quaver. "I'm looking for the gearshift."

He took her hand and placed it on the plastic knob. "Maybe you could be careful when you put this thing into second? This is a little cramped quarters."

She eased the stick back into gear and felt her thumb brush against the inside of his thigh. She closed her eyes in disbelief and scorching embarrassment. "This is impossible! Can't you scrinch into the seat a little?"

"I'm scrinched as much as I can scrinch. If you'd just get moving, you could put it into third, and we'd all feel better."

Chris spun the wheel and peeled out into the stream of traffic.

Ken Callahan gripped the dashboard. "Holy cow, now I know how you got all those dents in your car."

"Do you want to drive?"

"You wouldn't want to know what I'd like to do," he returned between clenched teeth.

Chris clutched the wheel with all the desperation of a drowning woman clinging to a leaking life preserver. She couldn't ever remember feeling so disturbed by a man. Every move she made pressed against hard muscle and sent suspicious sensations fluttering along her nerve endings, resulting in an odd mixture of fear, annoyance, and raw physical attraction. She focused her attention on the road and took a deep breath to steady herself. It was a ridiculous situation, and she knew it was going to get worse before it got better. She was up to fifty miles an hour and still driving in third gear. The motor whined in protest. She had to put the truck into fourth gear, but that meant sliding her hand along the inside of his right leg, again. *This is my punishment for neglecting my car,* she agonized. *I didn't feed it oil, and I lied to it, and the Car Fairy is getting even.*

Ken Callahan cleared his throat nervously. "Uh, you really should put it into fourth."

"I know that." She glanced at him in the rear-view mirror and realized he was biting back laughter. "Something funny?"

"You're kinda cute when you're all flustered."

She made a grunting sound of pure annoyance. The only thing worse than being flustered was having him know she was flustered. She wrapped her fist around the gearshift and plunged it back with a vengeance.

"*Yeow!*" he gasped, jumping out of the way and smashing the surprised dog against the car door. "Watch what you're doing with that thing. I hope to have children some day."

"If you make me any more nervous you're not going to live to have breakfast . . . much less children."

He settled into his seat, and Chris felt his eyes watching her speculatively. Embarrassment, and some other emotion she didn't care to analyze, rose in fiery waves clear to the roots of her hair.

He touched her flaming cheek with the back of his hand. "You're blushing."

She groaned inwardly. Blushing was an understatement. If her face got any hotter, she'd be able to fry an egg on her forehead.

"This is a first for me. I've never been able to make a woman blush. I didn't think modern women did that sort of thing." He wound his finger around an orange curl and tugged lightly. "It's nice." His voice was soft and low. It reminded Chris of fine brandy that had the unusual ability to simultaneously soothe and stimulate. "What's your name?"

"Chris Nelson."

"That's a very no-nonsense name for a slightly crazy lady. You look more like a Tootsie or a Fanny . . . or maybe a Lucy."

"Lucy is my daughter's name."

"You have a daughter?" There was a moment of pregnant silence while he digested the fact of her motherhood. "How old is she?"

"Seven."

"And her father?"

"Gone."

"Poor man. Life must always seem dull after living with you."

She gave him a sidewise glance and saw a smile threatening to emerge at the corners of his mouth.

Damn him. He was laughing at her again. How dare he enjoy himself when she was so uncomfortable. And he didn't even have the good grace to be obnoxious—the rat was downright adorable.

He shifted his broken arm, trying to find a more comfortable position. "Is it much farther?"

"The hospital turnoff is just ahead. Does your arm hurt?"

"It's down to a dull throb."

Chris had an insane urge to kiss his arm and make it better. Maternal instincts, she assured herself. Nothing more than a hormone imbalance left over from childbirth. The fact that he was incredibly handsome had nothing to do with it.

They were traveling down a four-lane highway with a safety island running down the middle. Chris pulled into the left-turn lane, stopped at the intersection, and watched the oncoming traffic. Rain pelted the windshield, making it difficult to see openings in the morning rush of commuters.

"Here we are," Chris announced, finally able to complete the turn. She pulled the truck into the brightly lit parking lot and rolled to a stop in a space near the emergency entrance.

Ken Callahan gave an audible sigh of relief. The Rottweiler looked around expectantly and thumped his tail against the upholstery.

For some reason Chris suddenly felt annoyed that everyone was so happy to have arrived at their destination. It was as if they were overjoyed at the prospect of quitting her company. Not very complimentary, especially since she was unaccountably depressed at the thought of leaving Ken Callahan. "Hmmph," she snapped.

"Hmmph?"

"You and your dog are obviously ecstatic to see my driving come to an end."

"You drive like a maniac. And besides, you've been fondling me for fifteen minutes. How much do you think a man can take?"

"Fondling you?" she squeaked. "Of all the . . . I never . . . you . . ."

"Oh, man, now I've got you all upset. Listen, I know this is a small truck, and you probably didn't mean to fondle me, but . . ."

"I don't drive like a maniac. I've never driven a truck before." She shook her finger at him. "You haven't made it any easier—you and your dumb dog—and let me assure you that if I fondled you it was purely accidental."

"Yeah, and it was accidental that you broke my arm," he teased.

"You didn't move fast enough!"

He grinned sheepishly. "You're right. I'm not at

my best this morning. I didn't get much sleep last night." He leaned toward her and nuzzled her hair. "It wasn't entirely my fault, you know. I was distracted. You looked downright wanton . . . leaning over the engine at me."

Wanton? Of all the nerve, she huffed to herself. She might have been ogling a little, but she definitely hadn't been wanton—had she? "I wasn't feeling wanton. I was concerned about my car."

"Your voice was husky." His lips brushed against her neck as he spoke. His warm breath whispered along tingling skin.

Chris felt her stomach lurch. "My voice is always husky in the morning," she lied. "I wasn't awake, yet. I didn't have time for coffee."

He kissed the nape of her neck, sending a shiver rocketing along her spine. He leaned against her and placed a nibbling sort of kiss just below her earlobe while rain drummed on the roof of the truck, wrapping them in cozy isolation. Chris wondered why she was sitting there, waiting to be kissed again. She had dated sporadically since her divorce, mostly to appease well-meaning friends, and she'd always found herself counting the minutes before she could issue the perfunctory goodnight kiss and get home to her daughter. *Why on earth am I feeling so attracted to this man? I don't even know him. I literally picked him up at the side of the road.* She felt a little hysterical.

Ken slipped his hand inside the red vest, his fingers curled around Chris's rib cage. "Chris Nelson," he whispered silkily, "you're a very dangerous lady." His thick black lashes lowered as his gaze dropped to her lips.

Chris felt her body turn toward him, desire creeping through her like heated honey. His lips grazed hers in a kiss that was featherlight and lingering.

"Mmmmm..." she purred—and then wondered who'd just made that incredibly contented sound. Surely, it wasn't Chris Nelson. Chris Nelson was a dedicated professional, an intrepid mother. Up to now, the only thing capable of evoking that sort of response in Chris Nelson was her mother's New York cheesecake. She sat up with a jolt, surprising both man and dog. The Rottweiler stopped panting momentarily and eyed her suspiciously.

Ken Callahan drew his eyebrows together in a small frown. "Now what?" he asked warily.

"You're trying to seduce me in a hospital parking lot."

"What's wrong with that?"

What's wrong with it is that it's working, she thought. "I don't even know you. And it's inappropriate.

And . . ." She was babbling. Grasping at straws. "And your dog is watching."

A look of disbelief registered on Ken Callahan's face. It changed to a smile. He tipped his head back and laughed triumphantly. "I'm really getting to you, huh?"

She pressed her lips together in annoyance. "Doesn't your arm hurt anymore?"

"Not nearly as much as my heart," he confessed playfully.

She opened the truck door and jumped out into the rain, ran the short distance to the emergency entrance, and stood just inside the lobby, shaking out her wet hair and stomping the water off her sneakered feet. She pointed toward the desk. "Why don't you go and register. I need to make a call. I'm late for work."

"It's five-thirty in the morning. What sort of job do you have? Delivering newspapers? Making doughnuts? Hit man for the mob on the early-morning shift?"

"I'm a skate coach. The rink opens at five-twenty so the kids can practice before school starts."

He studied her slim, compact body and nodded. "It's easy to imagine you on the ice. I'm afraid I'm not very knowledgeable about ice skating—are you famous?"

Chris paused to look at him. His eyes were guileless and filled with genuine curiosity. "I suppose I was several years ago, but I'm not any longer. I might have a certain amount of recognition among other skaters, but my name is hardly a household word these days." She realized she'd left her purse in the athletic bag in the truck and started a fruitless search through the pockets of her vest.

Ken placed his cell phone in the palm of her hand. "I assume this is what you're looking for." He grabbed her elbow as she turned away. "Get back to me as fast as you can," he pleaded, "I hate hospitals."

When Chris returned, she found Ken Callahan slouched in a chair, his long legs stretched in front of him. His arm had been put in a sling, and he looked up at her anxiously over a cup of coffee. "You've been gone for hours—what took you so long?"

"I've been gone for five minutes."

He smiled boyishly, slightly embarrassed. "Well, it seemed like hours. They've already taken X-rays." He pointed to a Styrofoam cup on the table beside him. "I got you some coffee."

Chris removed the lid and added a container of cream, then studied him as she sipped at the coffee. He had high cheekbones, a perfectly straight nose, and a few flecks of gray in the unruly profusion of wavy black hair. He had a wide mouth, which she could easily imagine set in ruthless determination, but right now he stared moodily into his coffee, the corners of his mouth turned down, and Chris wondered why he was looking so grim. "Is something wrong?"

"To tell you the truth . . . I'm scared to death. I've never been in a hospital before. And I've never broken anything that was mine. Will it hurt?"

Chris gaped in astonishment. He was serious. He really was scared. She smiled and shook her head. "I don't think it will hurt."

"Have you ever broken anything?"

"When I was a little girl we lived on a farm in Colorado—not a working farm, we just called it a farm because it was eleven acres, and it had a barn. When my parents bought the farm it came complete with a big old black horse named Looney. He was a great horse, but every now and then he liked to see me go over a fence solo. He'd run right up to a fence, plant his feet, and I'd go soaring off into the air. One time I crashed into a split rail and broke my nose."

Ken slowly ran the tip of his finger along the bridge of her nose. "It's a pretty little nose. Straight until the very end, where it tips up just a bit. Elegant without being boring."

She felt her heart flop at his touch, and an unaccountable tingle ran down her spine. "Mmmm," she answered, waiting for her mind to clear. "And then when I was eight I was dancing in my room with a laundry basket on my head . . . and I tripped over a roller skate and broke my arm."

"I find that surprisingly easy to believe."

"And when I was twelve, I broke my finger playing softball."

"Never been hurt skating?"

"Bruises. Lots of bruises. Nothing serious."

"Did you ever compete?"

"For years and years. I was National Novice champion at sixteen, Junior champion when I was eighteen, and National Senior bronze and silver medalist. And then I quit."

He watched her quietly. Their mutual silence grew uncomfortable, the inevitable question hanging ominously suspended in the air between them.

Chris sighed. "Don't you want to know why I quit? Everyone always does."

"I thought it might be sensitive."

She smiled at him, pleasantly surprised at his perception. "It was a long time ago. As a young athlete I'd led a very narrow life. Up at five in the morning. In bed by nine at night. I was the world's latest bloomer. I'd never had any sort of relationship with a boy until I was twenty-one. And that relationship resulted in my daughter, Lucy."

He drained his cup of coffee and returned it to the table. His hand found hers and traced a line along her ring finger. "Want to tell me about the father?"

"Steven Black."

He whistled softly. "The actor?"

"The classic whirlwind courtship. He wined and dined me for two weeks. I thought I was madly in love." She shrugged with her hand. "We were married in a thirty-second service in Las Vegas. Four weeks later I discovered I was pregnant, and my adoring husband divorced me while I was still in my first trimester."

He raised his eyebrows in astonishment. "Why did he do that?"

"Steven wanted a glamorous wife. If I'd stayed with skating I would have been on the Olympic team. Eight years ago Steven was still struggling for recognition, and I suppose he thought he could use the media coverage. When I refused to have an abortion and told him I was giving up competing, he divorced me."

Ken slid his hand along hers and gripped her

wrist. Little prickles of pleasure ran up her arm at his possessive touch. His hand was large—a working man's hand, she decided. Strong. Permanently tan. It was a hand that could be gentle and protective and still manipulate with confident authority. In a sudden flash of insight Chris knew what it would be like to share a bed with Ken Callahan. A burst of unexpected heat rushed through her at the thought, and a scarlet scald crept from her shirt collar.

Ken regarded her with serious curiosity. "It must have been difficult for you to give up competing."

Chris smiled. "It was easy. I loved to skate, but I hated to compete. I threw up before every competition. And as soon as I became pregnant my whole body oozed contentment." She sat forward in her seat, warming to her subject. "Having a baby is a miracle." Her face glowed with satisfaction and pride. "They have fat little hands and tiny fingernails, and they love you . . . just because you're there, and you're Mommy. Babies don't care if you're famous or rich."

She felt his hand tighten on hers and knew she had allowed some of the hurt of rejection to surface. She hadn't meant to show that to him. She hadn't even known herself that it still existed.

She hurried to cover the slip. "My favorite part of the day is when Lucy and I read bedtime stories. The book I like best is about this little bear. He gets a bicycle, and his father is going to teach him how to ride it, but the father does everything wrong! And then there's another Little Bear book where Little Bear and his dad go hiking with the bear scouts—" Chris stopped suddenly and closed her eyes with a groan. "I don't believe I'm telling you about Little Bear."

His voice was mockingly serious, but his dark eyes danced with amusement. "Little Bear is undoubtedly an important part of your life."

"Are you laughing at me again?"

He put his hand to her cheek. "No. I think it's very nice."

A white-coated intern appeared before them. "Mr. Callahan? I have the results of your X-rays. You have a simple fracture. It's not terribly serious, but it'll require a cast. You can go to an orthopedist of your choice, or I can have a staff doctor paged for you. I believe Dr. Wiley is on the floor somewhere."

"Dr. Wiley will be fine."

A bank of steel-gray clouds hung low in the early-morning sky, diffusing the sunlight and adding a chill to the air. Ken Callahan brandished his flourescent green, spanking-new cast, like a flag—holding it high to prevent his arm from swelling.

"Keep it above your heart for a few days," Dr. Wiley had advised.

"Above my heart," Ken mumbled, heading for his truck in long, angry strides. "Damned inconvenience." He stopped and looked down at his plaster-clad arm. The cast stretched from his elbow to the middle of his hand, wrapping around his thumb, and making it impossible to grasp anything with his left hand. He wiggled his fingers pathetically. "Just look at this," he ranted. "How can I drive? How can I work? How can I tie my damned shoes?"

Chris trotted beside him. She unlocked the doors to the truck and bit her lip to keep from laughing. Ken Callahan had ceased to frighten her. He wasn't as disreputable as she'd originally assumed. He was well-spoken and easy to talk to. A little over-sexed, perhaps, but not weird or dangerous. And she knew from the past two hours that his anger was short-lived. He was not a man that held a grudge or nursed a wound—and the memory of him locking her hand in a death grip while his cast was being applied sent spasms of laughter choking in her throat. Her hilarity ceased when she opened the door and came face-to-snout with the Rottweiler. There was a tug at Chris's vest collar and warm breath skimmed along her neck.

"I can hardly wait for fourth gear," Ken murmured into her ear.

"You weren't so crazy about fourth gear when we pulled in here."

"I was worried about being driven to the police station."

"And you're not worried anymore?"

"I've decided to take my chances."

Chris wrinkled her nose at him. "Well you needn't be concerned. It's light out. I can see what I'm doing, now. Your honor is perfectly safe." He was a nice man, but she was going to be extra careful about first gear. She didn't have the time or desire to complicate her life with a man. She slid behind the wheel and, after Ken was settled, turned to him. "I suppose I should drive you somewhere. Home? Or to work? Where were you going this morning?"

"I was starting a new job. I wanted to get in early and take a look around before anyone else showed up."

"Oh, no," she groaned, "first day on the job, and I broke your arm." She looked at the jeans and scuffed boots. He had removed his sweatshirt in deference to the cast, leaving him in a yellow short-sleeved T-shirt, which said CONSTRUCTION WORKERS USE THEIR TOOLS. The shirt clung to a flat stomach and broad, muscled chest, the sleeves spanning well-defined biceps. His forearm was corded, the back covered with a silk mat of black hair. There was no doubt in Chris' mind that he could crack a walnut as easily as an egg. Her eyes glazed over in silent admiration.

"Earth to Chris."

"Uh, I was just wondering about your shirt. You do construction work?"

"Yeah."

Not a laborer, she decided. He didn't seem the sort to take orders. A project manager or a supervisor, maybe. Certainly someone who worked in the field. He didn't get all those muscles sitting behind a desk. "Should I take you to work?"

He looked at the cast. "I think I'll pass on work today."

"Won't someone be upset if you don't show up?"

"Relieved would probably be a better word."

The truck idled at a standstill in the parking lot. "That's a strange thing to say. Are you insecure?" she joked.

He shook his head. "No. I'm ruthless."

An inadvertent shiver ran down her spine at the bitter tone in his voice.

"And I'm disreputable," he teased, trying to lighten the conversation.

"It's the stubble."

He rubbed his hand across his whiskered chin. "Twenty-eight of my last forty-eight hours have been spent on a plane. And only three of the remaining twenty hours were spent sleeping. I was afraid to take a razor to my face at four-thirty this morning."

"Where did you fly in from?"

"Everywhere."

She felt him slump in the seat next to her. He passed a hand through his hair and sighed. "I've been to three countries and seven cities in the last forty-eight hours. Six job sites. This would have been number seven. Maybe I'm glad you broke my arm. I think I'm running on empty."

"Are you some sort of troubleshooter?"

"Troubleshooter? I guess that's as good a name as any, but lately I feel more like a trouble*maker*." He quirked a smile at her. "I'd like to make a pass at you, but all of a sudden, I'm so tired I can hardly keep my eyes open."

"Would you like me to drive you home?"

"I don't think I have a home." It was a flat statement issued in a voice totally devoid of emotion.

"There's this place out in Loudoun County where I stay sometimes."

"Loudoun County! After I drop you off, how will I ever get back here? Loudoun County is miles away. There aren't any buses running to Loudoun County, there isn't a subway running to Loudoun County, what are you doing living in Loudoun County?"

He sat with his black curls resting against the rear window, his eyes closed in exhaustion, his cast propped in a ridiculous position on the head of the Rottweiler. "You could spend the night," he smiled dreamily. "It's lonely in Loudoun County."

"I'll pass on the night stuff, but I guess I can drive you home. After all, you did try to help me."

"Mmmmm."

Chris glanced at her watch. "I have students waiting for me right now. Would you mind hanging around at the skating rink for a couple hours? I'll be done at ten-thirty, and then I can make arrangements with one of the other coaches to follow us out and bring me back home."

"Mmmmm."

Chris looked at him suspiciously. "Did you hear anything I said?" There was no response. He was asleep.

Chapter 2

Chris dried her skate blades and put the custom Harlicks in her locker. She slipped her feet into her tennis shoes and wondered about the man and dog she'd left slumbering in the parking lot. She'd treated them equally, cracking a window for ventilation and covering them with a blanket from the coaches' lounge. Toward the end of her last lesson she'd had visions of man and beast perishing—like the little match girl—frozen to death under a mantle of dog-induced frost. She pushed through the heavy lobby door and stared horrified into the parking lot. There was no truck. There was no trace of Ken Callahan. No dog.

Bitsy Schoffit barged through the doors behind her. "Okay, I'm ready to go."

Chris spread her arms in a gesture of confusion. "He isn't here. The truck is gone."

"I thought he couldn't drive."

"I dunno. Maybe he called someone to come

and get him while I was on the ice." She clapped her hand to her forehead. "And he's got my purse. I left it in the truck."

Bitsy shook her head and made motherly clucking sounds with her tongue. "Dumb, dumb, dumb."

"It's not so bad. He probably got someone to take him home and didn't realize the purse was on the floor. I'll just go home and call the hospital. Maybe someone there can get in touch with him."

Bitsy unlocked the door to her BMW, motioned for Chris to get in, and plunked her own small body into the plush red seat. At forty-three she was still slim and graceful on ice, moving effortlessly with her students through difficult choreography. On land she was an ox. On land she stomped and plunked and stumbled with unconscious abandon.

Bitsy turned the BMW onto Little River Turnpike. Half a mile up the road the two women simultaneously spotted Chris' abandoned tan hatchback on the far shoulder. They gave it a cursory glance, as if it belonged to some unknown person, and continued on to the next light.

"Old news," Chris said finally—her thoughts returning to the car.

Bitsy was familiar with the Chris Nelson philosophy of car care. "Time to buy a new one, huh?"

"Five weeks too early. I have my money tied up in a savings bond that doesn't mature for five more weeks."

Bitsy gave another series of clucks. "Tsk, tsk, tsk." She pulled into Chris' subdivision and rolled to a stop in front of her house. "Let me guess," she said, pointing to the blue pickup parked at the curb. "Is this the phantom truck?"

"Oh no! What's he doing here?"

Bitsy chuckled. "I imagine he's in there having tea with Aunt Edna."

"Just what I need. Edna's convinced I should remarry. Remember poor John Farrell? And last week she arranged a date for me with the guy who came to read our electric meter. Edna'll take one look at Ken Callahan and think she's gone to matchmakers' heaven."

"Wow. That nice?"

"An eleven, no sweat. And I don't want to have anything to do with him. I like my life just the way it is." Chris slammed the car door behind her and took twelve feet of sidewalk in two strides. She turned, waved at Bitsy, and hammered on her front door.

Aunt Edna bellowed, "Hold your pants on," and glared out above a security chain. "Well, good golly," she complained, "what with all that thundering, I thought it had to be some lunatic escaped from Lorton prison. Why didn't you just use your key?"

"It's in my purse, and I don't have my purse with me." Chris pushed past Edna. "Where is he?"

"You mean that nice Ken Callahan?"

Chris moved from the foyer to the living room, to the dining room. She felt her patience evaporating and clenched her teeth to keep from shouting. "Yes. 'That nice Ken Callahan.' Where is he?"

Aunt Edna blocked the doorway between living room and dining room. She stood five feet tall in sensible sturdy brown shoes, and her snow-white hair was tightly curled in rows marching obediently across her gleaming pink skull. She had snapping blue eyes—and a body like a fireplug. "It was just like Goldilocks," she cried, slapping her leg. "I took Lucy to school, and when I came home there he was—sleeping in your bed."

Chris felt her voice rise to a shriek. "In my bed?"

"He's such a nice man, dear. And he looked so peaceful, tucked under your big down quilt."

Her eyes widened in a mixture of outrage and disbelief. "Under my quilt?"

The stairs creaked behind Chris, and she whirled around as Ken sauntered into the room, looking sleepily sexy and perfectly at home.

"I don't know how two tiny women can make so much noise," he mumbled. "What's all the racket about?"

"*You!* How did you get in here? And what were you doing in my bed?"

He rubbed the back of his neck and grinned. Evidently remembering his cast, he diligently raised it above his heart. "Dog and I just about froze to death in the truck. I was going to come inside the skating rink to get warm, but I was afraid I looked too disreputable, so I fished around in your purse until I found your address and your keys, and then I drove myself over here."

"I thought you couldn't drive."

"Well, I discovered I could just about wrap my fingers around the wheel." He waved his cast at her and wiggled his fingers. "And lucky it was my left arm that you broke, because I can shift with my good hand."

"And then you just let yourself in and went to bed?" she sputtered.

"There wasn't anyone home. I put Dog in your backyard and went upstairs."

"It was just like Goldilocks," Aunt Edna insisted. "I went upstairs and there he was, sleeping just as peaceful as could be."

"Until Edna started screaming." He raised an eyebrow at Edna. "You've got some voice."

Edna sniffed indignantly. "Well, what do you think? You think I'm some frail old lady? And if you hadn't come up with a good explanation I'd have cracked your skull wide open with my wooden rolling pin."

Chris smiled and looked sidewise at Ken. "Don't doubt it for a minute," she whispered.

"You're obviously closely related."

"Aunt Edna is my mother's sister and reigning family matriarch."

"Seventy-five years old, and I'm almost as good as new," she said proudly. "Now you young folks go into the parlor, and I'll get us some refreshments."

"That won't be necessary, Aunt Edna. I'm sure Mr. Callahan will be anxious to be on his way."

Aunt Edna's mouth closed with a determined snap. "I won't hear of it. Anyone can see the man is hungry, and he don't look like he's in such a hurry to leave."

Ken beamed. "I'd like to stay for refreshments."

"You see?" Edna gloated. "I knew he didn't want to rush off." She smacked her lips with satisfaction and bustled off to the kitchen.

Ken smiled. "I like your aunt."

Chris glanced up at him. "When my marriage collapsed it was Aunt Edna that put the pieces back together. Her own husband died eleven years ago. When I was in my eighth month, Aunt Edna arrived unannounced and informed me that I needed looking after. I was the only one in my Lamaze class with a sixty-seven-year-old lady for a coach." Chris shook her head, still amazed at the memory. "She went right through delivery with me. She was wonderful."

"And she's lived with you ever since?"

"Off and on. She travels from family member to family member. Mostly wherever there's a disaster. Lately I've tried to keep her here because of Lucy. In order for me to make enough money to support us it's necessary for me to give after-school and evening lessons. If it weren't for Aunt Edna, I'd have to put Lucy in day care and hire babysitters at night."

Ken relaxed onto the couch and patted the spot next to him. "Come sit by me." The sounds of banging cupboards and clanking dishes drifted in from the kitchen. Ken looked in the direction of the clatter. His mouth twitched and finally gave way to a full-fledged grin.

"What's so funny?"

"I just thought of something your aunt said to me." He threw his head back and laughed.

Chris marveled at the quality of his laughter. It was full and rich and deeply masculine and impossible to ignore. She smiled and prodded him. "Well? What did she say?"

"When she walked in and found me asleep in your bed, she let out with this ear-splitting screech—it had me sitting bolt upright before I even opened my eyes. But then she took a good look at me. I guess she sized me up and figured I was okay, because her first words were . . . 'Merciful heavens, there's finally a man in my niece's bed.'"

"I'll kill her."

"I get the impression that your aunt would like to see you married."

"That's the understatement of the century. She's fixed me up with meter readers, shoe salesmen, a fat fifty-two-year-old butcher, and last week she scared the bejeebers out of John Farrell."

"Who's John Farrell?"

"My accountant." Chris waved her hand in a dismissing gesture. "As soon as Aunt Edna found out John was single she did everything but produce my dental records and promise a dowry. I love Aunt Edna, but she's entirely guileless, and she gets more outspoken as she gets older. She says she hasn't got much time left, so she's not going to spend it pussyfooting around."

"Edna ever find John Farrell in your bed?"

"No!" Chris rolled her eyes at the thought. She couldn't imagine pleasant, innocuous John Farrell in her bed. She took a stealthy breath and reluctantly admitted to herself that she could easily imagine Ken Callahan there.

Edna trotted in with a plate of cookies. "Are you talking about that John Farrell?" She narrowed her eyes at Ken. "What a wimp. Had him over to dinner and he picked at his roast beef. Didn't eat his peas at all." She shook her head in dismay. "That man had no spirit. No backbone." She winked at Ken and smiled broadly at Chris. "Now this one here is more like it. This guy's got something to him."

Chris sighed and selected a cookie. Once Aunt Edna got started there was no stopping her. Might as well sit back and watch him squirm, she thought, taking a perverse delight in the possibility that Ken and Edna deserved each other. After all, it wasn't as if she had any future plans for Ken Callahan. She wouldn't ever see him again—might as well let Aunt Edna have some fun with him.

"Are you married?" Edna asked.

"Nope."

Edna looked appalled. "A big, strapping man like you—not married? And you're not getting any younger. How old are you?"

"Thirty-six."

Edna took an Oreo. She broke it in half and nibbled the white icing off one of the wafers. "You're not one of those men that prefers boys, are you?"

Ken choked on his Ovaltine. "No ma'am! I'm . . . uh . . . old-fashioned about that kind of stuff."

Chris covered her mouth to keep from laughing. This promised to be even better than the demolition of John Farrell.

Edna leaned forward in eager anticipation. "You got a steady job?"

Ken turned to Chris; his eyes danced with diabolical delight. The silent message was blatant: Feed me to the wolves, will you? When he turned back to Edna his face was a solemn mask. "I was supposed to start a new job today, but as you can see . . ." He waved his arm pathetically in front of him. "I've got a broken arm. I can't work with this cast on."

Edna sucked in her breath. "And all because you stopped to help my niece. Isn't that noble? Don't that beat all?"

Chris pressed herself deeper into the sofa cushions and surreptitiously made a motion that said she might gag. "Noble," she croaked.

Ken stole a smug look in Chris' direction. He toyed with a vanilla wafer.

"What a pity," Edna went on. "How will you get by?"

"I have some savings."

"A man with a savings account. Now that's character," she told her niece. "Seems a shame to have to dip into your savings on account of us. I feel just terrible about this."

A knot was developing in Chris' stomach. This wasn't taking the usual course. By this time Aunt Edna should have had him in a sweat, but Ken was looking more pleased by the minute. And he was planning something sneaky—Chris was sure of it.

Ken stretched and relaxed deeper into the couch. "This is a nice room."

Chris blinked at the sudden change in conversation. There was none of the earlier affectation. He seemed genuinely impressed. *I don't trust him,* she thought. He'd been leading up to something. She sat up warily and paid close attention, watching his eyes as they observed the room.

It was an airy room with ivory walls and

matching sheers. The plush wall-to-wall carpeting was a warm beige tone. The few pieces of furniture were comfortably overstuffed and covered in earth-tone tans with the exception of a cocoa-and-white houndstooth check wingback chair. The subdued colors provided the perfect background for gregarious Boston ferns, delicate asparagus ferns, potted fig trees, basketed orange trees, hanging ivies, and a colorful collection of African violets in traditional clay pots. The plants seemed to begin in the living room, randomly sprinkled here and there, picking up momentum and becoming more dense as they progressed toward the dining room, where they converged around the patio doors.

Ken's attention focused on a cluster of photographs hanging on the wall. "Do you mind if I look at the pictures in your dining room?"

Aunt Edna jumped to her feet. "You want to see the pictures?"

Chris groaned. This was not a good sign.

"This here's a photograph of some sailing ships. Chris got this when we went vacationing in Maine last year. And this here's a picture of me when I was a little girl. Wasn't I a pip? Just look at those ribbed stockings. This is an elephant at the zoo, and this is a picture Lucy drew when we came home."

Ken looked at the crayon drawing of a smiling elephant. It had been framed and matted with the same professional care as all the other pictures. He tilted his head in Chris' direction. "Your daughter must feel very special to have her drawing on this wall."

Chris caught her breath at the enigmatic softening in his eyes, the tender huskiness of his voice.

Edna puffed up with pride. "It's a beauty of an elephant, isn't it? She can draw anything. She's got real talent."

"Like her mom." Ken smiled at Edna.

"The spitting image." Edna pointed to a photograph of a little girl hanging upside down from a tree limb. Her orange hair hung in wild curls that hadn't seen a comb all day. She wore pink shorts, smudged with mud. Her sneakers were battered, her shoelaces untied, and she was laughing and closing her eyes tight in childish abandon.

Ken laughed with the photograph. "Is this Lucy?"

"Yep. But it might as well have been her mother. She looked just like that when she was seven."

His attention wandered to the bowl of cut flowers in the middle of the dining room table. He ran his finger over the table's freshly polished surface.

"You've done a lot to make this a home. I wish I had a home like this."

Little alarm bells sounded in Chris' brain. There was a genuine wistfulness to his voice, which she didn't doubt, but his eyes were filled with mischief and cunning.

"Haven't you got a home?" Edna exclaimed.

He shook his head. "I've been doing a lot of traveling because of my job. I haven't had much time to gather the things together that make a house a home."

"Maybe Chris could help you. Where do you live? Do you have a house of your own?"

"There's this place out in Loudoun County where I stay sometimes."

"Loudoun County. That's a ride."

He nodded. "It would be much more convenient for me if I lived around here." He delicately draped his good arm around Edna's shoulders. "I have a confession to make. Ever since I walked into this house, I've been toying with an idea. I have two problems—I haven't got a homey place to live, and I can't go to work for a while. You and Chris also have two problems—you haven't got a car, and you haven't got an abundance of money. I noticed that you have an extra bedroom and bath downstairs—maybe we could work out some kind of deal. The use of my truck, plus"—he waved his hand while he contemplated a sum—"fifty dollars a week. We could be roomies."

Chris sprang from the couch. *"No!"*

Edna stood firm with her hands on her hips. "I think it's a wonderful idea."

"We don't even know this man."

"I know all I need to know. This house needs a man underfoot." Edna smacked her lips and narrowed her eyes in determination. "Do you take out garbage?" she asked Ken.

"Yes, ma'am."

"You see?" she informed her niece. "He'll be perfect."

"He'll be a perfect pain in the . . ."

Edna raised her eyebrows in warning. She didn't allow any cussing.

". . . in the foot. And what about Lucy?"

Now Ken raised his eyebrows. "What about Lucy?"

"It wouldn't look right."

"Pshaw," Edna scoffed. "Women have been taking in boarders for centuries."

Chris glared at the man standing smugly in front of her. "I would like to speak with you privately, in the kitchen," she hissed.

"Will you excuse us?" he said pleasantly to Aunt Edna.

Chris growled and stomped off to the kitchen. She closed the louvered kitchen door with a slam and turned to face Ken. "Let's get something perfectly straight, Ken Callahan. I have no intention of allowing you to live in this house. I think it's despicable of you to wheedle your way around my Aunt Edna, and I wouldn't trust you for a second with my daughter."

An expression of amused disgust played on his face. "That's a bunch of baloney. Your Aunt Edna is a nice old barracuda who only gets wheedled when she wants to. And it's not your daughter you're worried about—it's you."

Chris pressed her lips together in annoyance. He was right. She'd had a nice sane life—until this morning—and she didn't want it disrupted. And Ken could definitely disrupt. He was much too handsome. Much too sexy. And every now and then there was a flash of genuine vulnerability that broke down all her defenses. She had avoided romantic entanglements for the last seven years without feeling any real sense of loss. It was safe. It was comfortable. It was a way of life that would crumble with Ken lurking in her kitchen—wearing those formfitting faded jeans. She decided to take the coward's way out and ignore his accusations. She rallied to a new attack. "Why are you doing this?"

"I need a place to live."

"There are dozens of ads in the paper every day looking for roommates."

"That's true, but I like it here." He surveyed the kitchen, his gaze drifting from the blond butcher-block countertops with the brown teddy bear cookie jar and the assortment of clear glass jars filled with spaghetti, sugar, whole oats, macaroni, popcorn, and flour to a Peter Rabbit place setting stacked in the sink. A bulletin board and chalkboard had been hung on one wall—the chalkboard was at the proper height for a seven-year-old. Ken picked up a piece of colored chalk and drew a straight line across the green surface. He studied the line for a moment, seemingly intrigued by the textured mark. Almost reluctantly, he returned the chalk to its wooden carrier and turned to Chris, putting his hand on her shoulder in a possessive caress that lingered briefly then moved to her neck. His finger touched an earlobe and slid along the curve of her jaw. "And I like you. I don't know why. You're kind of crusty. And you're too skinny. But there's something about you that makes my toes curl."

"What do you mean crusty and skinny? I'm not at all crusty, and I'm certainly not skinny."

He stepped closer, smiling broadly, obviously pleased that he'd provoked her. Chris felt the warmth from his body swirl around her, and the kitchen temperature seemed to rise twenty degrees. He continued to trail a path along her chin. When his finger reached her mouth, she instinctively licked her dry lips. Their reactions were totally different but equally swift. Chris jumped away as if she'd been burned. How could less than five seconds of contact do that to her stomach? It was like falling forty floors in an elevator.

Ken Callahan's stomach seemed to be made of sterner stuff. He smiled wolfishly and pressed himself against her, pinning her to the wall. "I realize that lovely little lick was just a reflex action, but I'm going to take advantage of it anyway," he whispered cheerfully.

"Don't you dare!"

"I can't help myself. Kitchens always have this romantic effect on me."

"Keep away from me, or I'll bop you on the head with Aunt Edna's rolling pin."

"Wouldn't you like to be kissed in the kitchen?" he teased.

"No."

"Are you sure? I'm a terrific kisser."

The man is evil, Chris decided. *He knows he can raise my blood pressure just by dropping his voice an octave, and he's absolutely enjoying it.* She pushed against his chest with both hands, hoping he wouldn't feel her heart pounding in her chest. "You're horrid."

"I like when your voice gets all husky and tremulous like that." His cobalt eyes lowered as he played with the zipper on her sweat suit jacket. "There's a nice chemistry between us. You knew it as soon as I did—when we looked at each other under the hood of your car. For some reason it scares the heck out of you."

"I don't want to get involved."

"I know that. That's why I'm moving in."

"*What?*"

"If I did the normal thing and asked you out to dinner, would you go out with me?"

"No."

"I didn't think so. So I'll live here." He smoothed the rumples from the front of her warm-up suit. "Besides, it will be convenient for both of us. I really do need a place to stay. I'm tired of shifting around. I need a home—even if it's someone else's home. And you need the money and the transportation. A match made in heaven."

Oh boy, she thought, *I'm doomed. Putty in his hands.* "Do you know what a glamus is?"

"A what?"

"Never mind. I suppose you can stay." She sighed. "Aunt Edna has her mind made up, anyway." Suddenly she felt very, very tired. "But I'm serious about not getting involved. Keep your distance."

"Or you'll drive me straight to the police station."

Chris felt her lips twitch in spite of herself. "You're laughing at me, again."

"Maybe a little." His hand touched her waist and boldly slid under the jacket of her warm-up suit. He flattened his palm against her stomach. His eyes grew dark and liquid. "But it's a nice kind of laughing."

She knew it was a nice kind of laughing. It was gentle and good-humored and affectionate ... very affectionate. He was everything she didn't want to find in a man. He was lovable. And the feel of his hand on her stomach was exquisite. She was sure that when he removed the hand she would be branded for life—that she would never forget the delicious sensations emanating through her body.

There was a flurry of obtrusive plate clanking and throat clearing in the living room. "What's going on in there?" Edna called. "It's awfully quiet."

Ken deposited a quick, light kiss on Chris' lips and the muted hunger in his eyes shifted to amusement. "I don't think you have to worry about this arrangement. I think Aunt Edna could be a formidable chaperone."

Aunt Edna bustled through the kitchen door, the plates and glasses clattering noisily in her hands. "I hate being left out of stuff. If you're going to talk in the kitchen, then you're going to have to talk louder."

Chris took the dishes and began stacking them in the dishwasher. "We were just coming to terms with this—boarding arrangement."

Ken managed to steal a cookie before they were whisked away into the teddy bear cookie jar. "The deal is that I take out the garbage, and I mind my manners."

Aunt Edna nodded in approval. "Dinner is at six. You can have the run of the refrigerator between meals—as long as you don't eat us out of house and home. Goodness, it's nice to have a man in the house." She grinned.

Chris took a key from a hook on the bulletin board. She studied the key for a moment, contemplating the significance of the act. She suspected she was giving Ken more than just the key to her house. She was giving him the chance to wreak havoc with her life—and she didn't doubt for a second that he would take advantage of the opportunity. So, *why am I doing this?* she agonized. *Because I need his truck,* she answered. *Because I need his money.* Chris considered the key innocently resting in the palm of her hand. Were there other reasons? Because he was incredibly handsome? Because he could be outrageously endearing? *Because when he's close to me it's like lying in the sun—all sizzling skin and luscious heat that sinks straight to my soul.* Chris made an effort to control the shiver that ran along her spine, and presented him with the key. "This is for the front door."

Ken extracted a key ring from his jeans pocket and attempted to work a key loose. The key ring fell from his hand and clattered onto the kitchen floor. There was a brief look of dismay at his one-handed helplessness. He sighed and retrieved the keys. "And this is for the truck," he told her, handing her the entire key chain. He lowered his voice to a coaxing whisper. "I'm sorry, Chris, I can't do this by myself. You're going to have to help me."

She felt her pulse falter as she fumbled with the keys. Her eyes avoided his while she wrestled with the double entendre.

"Ain't that nice," Aunt Edna said. "A real ceremony. Just like getting married."

Chris felt heat creep along the back of her neck. Aunt Edna had the unnerving habit of saying out loud what everyone else was thinking. Chris thought back to the white-gowned pomp of her hastily planned wedding ceremony almost eight years ago. It had been lovely and exciting, but it had lacked the intimacy and intriguing solemnity of this simple kitchen key exchange. It was a frightening and annoying admission to make, but in some inexplicable way, she suddenly felt married to Ken Callahan.

Ken looked at the two women from under lowered lids as he returned his keys to his pocket. His mouth was stretched into a roguish smile that didn't quite extend to his tired eyes. "I don't think I'd make much of a bridegroom today, Aunt Edna. My arm is starting to ache again, and I'm exhausted."

"Land sakes, you look like you haven't slept in days."

"I haven't." He slouched against the doorjamb and hugged his broken arm. "Don't suppose you'd want to tuck me in?" he asked Chris.

Aunt Edna shook her head. "He sounds frisky, but he doesn't look like he has much spunk left in him. Why don't you show him his room while I fix lunch."

Chris led the way downstairs. The lower level rooms were carpeted in the same plush beige. A comfortably plump russet-colored corduroy couch, bordered by two end tables, faced the large brick fireplace that dominated a corner of the rec room. An oversized coffee table, overflowing with children's books, filled the space between the couch and the fireplace. Two doors led off the family room, one leading to a neat utility room, and the second leading to the guest bedroom and adjoining bath. Chris motioned to the double bed covered with a red plaid comforter. "There are fresh sheets on the bed. I'll bring some extra towels down later."

"Will you read me a bedtime story?" His voice was pleasantly husky with fatigue. "The one about Little Bear?"

Chris touched her finger to his bearded cheek. He was dead on his feet, but he could dredge up enough energy for some gentle teasing. Most men would be grouchy and short-tempered by now. There was something about him—a playfulness, a fleeting glimpse of wistful trust that stirred feelings in her that she'd only before felt for baby birds, orphaned kittens, and sleeping children. It was strange that the most virile, competent male she'd ever met could evoke such tender emotions.

Her eyebrows drew together in a scowl. And then there were the times when he was infuriating. Arrogant. Aggressive. Sneaky.

Ken shook his head. "I wouldn't want to guess what just went through your mind. I've never seen emotions parade across anyone's face like that before. One minute you were on the verge of a good night kiss and in a matter of seconds you were considering homicide."

"You're pretty sharp when you're tired."

He flopped down on the bed. "Mmmm, and I'm even better when I'm horizontal."

"You're impossible." Her mood seesawed back to poignant affection. "I'm sorry I broke your arm."

He closed his eyes and smiled. "I'm not."

Chris resisted the urge to help him with his boots. She turned quickly and left the room before he could open his eyes and see the glow of pleasure his words had produced.

Chapter 3

Chris sat in evening rush-hour traffic, one hand resting on the leather-wrapped steering wheel of Ken's custom truck, the other hand pressing against her churning stomach. She'd done something incredibly stupid. She'd allowed Ken into her house—into her heart. She would have been better off if she'd simply allowed him into her bed. That would have been sex. That would have been something she could handle.

She inched the truck forward in the endless traffic and slumped in her seat. Who was she trying to kid? Sex with Ken would be a disaster. *I'm like a dinosaur. I'm practically an extinct species. I'm a mental virgin, for Pete's sake.* She couldn't even imagine casual sex. And even if she could divorce sex from love, sex with Ken would probably ruin her for life—how would she ever top it?

Chris turned left off Little River Turnpike and headed for her subdivision. Her street looked normal enough. Her town house seemed just as she'd left it, but she knew it was merely a deceptive facade. Nothing would be normal as long as Ken had the key to her front door. She parked at the curb and tried to squelch the turmoil in her chest. *This will never work,* she told herself as she hopped from the truck. *He has to go.* She stomped up the sidewalk, berating herself. "How could I ever have agreed to this?" she muttered, throwing her arms in the air. "This is absurd." The front door crashed open and Chris stormed into the room.

"Well, here she is," Aunt Edna said to Ken. "Just like I told you. Muttering and stomping. All in a dither. Just look at her. Ain't she a pip?"

The last sentence was uttered with such unadulterated pride and love that Ken had to smile in appreciation. He adjusted the little girl on his lap to a more comfortable position and carefully laid a picture book on the coffee table.

Lucy smiled happily and held out her arms for her hello kiss. "Mommy, you're just in time to hear Ken finish the story."

Chris tipped her head in Ken's direction and gave him her most withering stare. "Little Bear?"

"Uh, no. I tried that, but I didn't feel entirely comfortable with a bunch of bears. I found one about a steam shovel. It's about this guy and his old steam shovel, and they've got to finish this job by sundown or . . ." Ken paused. "I suppose you already know the story," he added with an embarrassed grin.

I'm in big trouble, Chris thought. No woman in her right mind could hold out against that grin, and how could she possibly evict a man when he had her daughter enthralled on his lap? She bolstered her flagging hostility with the thought that this was just a temporary setback. She would kick him out after supper. She would do it the sneaky way—when Lucy and Aunt Edna were in bed and couldn't come to his rescue. Chris walked cautiously across the room to receive her daughter's hug, noting that the afternoon nap had erased the dark circles around Ken's eyes, and the tension lines had faded from his bearded cheeks. The corners of his mouth twitched with suppressed deviltry. There was no need for him to speak—his crackling blue eyes told her he had won this round and was openly gloating over his victory.

Chris bent to kiss her daughter's orange curls and upturned nose, unavoidably coming inches from Ken's freshly washed hair. She recognized the lemon-and-lilac scent. He had used her shampoo and bath soap. She paused for a moment, astonished at the wifely feelings this knowledge produced. It seemed perfectly natural and surprisingly intimate. A pang of longing for crushed dreams pierced her heart. It was such a simple thing—the intermingling of male and female fragrance. Emotions long buried were evoked and produced a pain that lodged in her throat like a huge silent sob.

She had always imagined that her marriage would be long and happy—like her parents'—a collection of shared intimacies, communal goals, loving memories. She had jumped at the first man who'd come along because she'd wanted all those things so badly. And she'd ended up with nothing.

No, that wasn't true. She had Lucy. And Lucy had been enough until this Ken Callahan had popped into her life. Damn him. Ken resurrected tender, hungry feelings that couldn't be trusted. He had the potential to be heartache and grief—and trouble with a capital T.

"This is ridiculous," she mumbled gruffly.

Ken chuckled at her exclamation. His laughter rumbled warm against her ear, and he feathered a kiss against her hair as she bowed her head to hug Lucy. "I'm not sure I follow you," he teased. "Care to elaborate?"

"This whole thing is ridiculous," she hissed in a stage whisper. "And I'll tell you more of what I'm talking about after supper."

She stiffened her back and fled to the kitchen to sort out her emotions. What was wrong with her? How could she be feeling so comfortably bound to a man that she'd picked up on the highway twelve hours ago? And if she did feel so comfortably bound to him, why did he make her so *un*comfortable? The answer to that was obvious. Because he was slick and handsome and too good to be true; another Prince Charming. A Steven Black clone. She pulled four plates from the kitchen cabinet and marched into the dining room. She thumped them on the table.

Lucy, still on Ken's lap, giggled. "Isn't Mommy funny when she's mad? She always makes so much noise."

Chris glared at the two of them, and Ken suppressed a smile. "Maybe we'd better finish this book," he suggested tactfully.

Chris made a frustrated gesture as she swished back through the kitchen doors. Twelve hours ago she'd picked up a construction worker on the highway and now he was living in her house and reading books about steam shovels to her daughter—and very shortly they'd all be sitting around feeling used and abandoned. Chris thrashed around in the silverware drawer. Everyone liked him. Aunt Edna liked him. Lucy liked him. She had to admit it—she even liked him. Why couldn't he have been some frog? Someone everyone hated. Someone that would have been easy to get rid of.

Aunt Edna turned from the stove with a disapproving look for the havoc Chris was causing among the silverware. She paused for effect, her wooden spoon held at half-mast. "He fits right in, don't he?"

"Mmmph," Chris gurgled, an expletive strangling in her throat. "I don't want him to fit right in. I want him to leave. I liked my life the way it was . . . without a man in my house."

Aunt Edna plopped her spoon back into the spaghetti sauce. "Nonsense. You've lived without a man long enough. Lucy needs a father, and you need a husband."

"I've already had a husband, and I didn't like it."

"That horse's rump wasn't a husband. Spent the whole day looking in the mirror, fixing his hair."

"What makes you think Ken's any better?"

The old woman wiped her hands on her apron and faced her niece. "I'm not real book smart, and every now and then I worry I'm getting a little senile, but I've got some common sense, and I know something about people. Ken Callahan is a good man. He's got gentleness and humor." Edna turned back to the stove, then shot her niece a sidewise look and smiled broadly. "And he's got a great body."

"Aunt Edna!"

"I might be old, but I know a great body when I see one. Uh-huh!"

Chris threw her head back and burst out laughing. She crossed the kitchen and hugged her aunt. "You're right, as always—he does have a great body."

Ken pushed through the kitchen door and snatched a breadstick from the glass jar on the counter. "So, you think I have a great body, huh?"

Chris grimaced. "God is really out to get me today."

"Don't be blasphemous," Edna warned.

Ken looked sadly at the cast on his arm. "My body used to be perfect."

I don't doubt it for a second, Chris thought.

"This is the second time I've had spaghetti today," Lucy announced. "We had spaghetti for lunch in school." She looked at the plate in front of her, piled with whole-wheat spaghetti noodles and Aunt Edna's chunky homemade sauce. Lucy sprinkled the freshly grated parmesan cheese on her meal with painstaking care. "The spaghetti we had in school was yucky. The noodles were white . . . like dead worms. And it didn't have any sausage in it or nothing. And the sauce was orange and watery. And I didn't eat it."

Ken nodded sympathetically. "What did you do with it, if you didn't eat it?"

Lucy looked at him suspiciously. "How do you know I did something with it?"

"Lucky guess."

Lucy giggled. "I gave it to Tommy Hostrup. Beth Ann Cristo gave hers to him. And Sally Winthrop. And Audrey Schtek. We gave him all our spaghetti, and we told him we'd give him a dollar if he could eat it."

"Did he eat it?"

"He tried, but he couldn't get it all in. It was awful. There were noodles hanging out of his mouth, and he had sauce all down his neck."

"When I was your age they served spaghetti in my school cafeteria, too," Ken told her. "We used to empty our milk cartons and fill them with the spaghetti. Then we'd take the cartons and put them behind the wheel of the principal's station wagon. When he drove away at the end of the day, he'd run over the cartons and all the spaghetti would squish out."

"Oh, gross!"

Ken leaned across the table and whispered to her conspiratorially. "There was this big bully in my school, Larry Newfarmer. He was really fat, and he used to pick on all the little kids. Everybody hated him. One day when we had spaghetti, I got his spelling workbook and put spaghetti noodles between all the pages without him knowing it."

Lucy's eyes got wide, and she clapped a hand over her mouth to control the giggles. "Then what?"

Ken leaned back in his chair and grinned sheepishly. "Then I sat on it. And the noodles got smashed between the pages. And when Larry Newfarmer went to spelling the next morning, those pages were stuck together forever."

Aunt Edna had bent her head and tried not to laugh. "Sh-sh-shame on you!" she managed when she was finally able to speak.

Chris' mouth curved into an unconscious smile. Her family was thoroughly enjoying Ken, and he seemed to be enjoying them. Other male guests had always politely tolerated Lucy—Ken actually liked her. He had a place in his heart for childish activities. *That's a nice trait to find in a man,* she thought, watching him in open admiration. He was lean and hard with broad shoulders and muscles in all the right places—but it was his face that intrigued her the most. There was an inherent strength in it. A magnetic confidence that could only be found in a man who had come to terms with himself and was not unhappy with what he saw. The fledgling beard enhanced the aura of virility that radiated from compelling blue eyes and a wide mobile mouth. An easy man to fall in love with, she mused . . . if you were the sort of woman who wanted to fall in love.

Ken raised a forkful of spaghetti to his lips and caught Chris watching him. His eyes searched her face, reaching into her thoughts. She decided to partially oblige him. "I was thinking about Mike Mulligan. You really enjoyed that, didn't you?"

The tips of his ears reddened. "I . . . uh . . . I've always liked steam shovels."

There was a loud rapping at the front door followed by a mournful howl.

Ken looked puzzled. "That sounds like Dog, but I know I left him in the backyard."

Edna got to the door first. "Well, Mrs. Thatcher," she smiled, opening the door wide.

Mrs. Thatcher stood flat-footed and ready for battle on the porch. She held the cowering Rottweiler by the collar. "Someone told me this dog came from the truck parked in front of your house. Is this your dog, Edna?"

"I don't know. What's he done?"

"He's destroyed every bush in my yard chasing rabbits, that's what he's done."

"Then he ain't my dog," Edna told her.

Ken took Edna by the shoulders and removed her from his path. "That's my dog, Mrs. Thatcher."

The huge black beast looked at his owner mournfully. Telltale sprigs of evergreen and pieces of bark clung from his collar.

"I'll be living here for a while," he told the woman. "Have the landscaping repaired, and I'll pay for it."

"Hmmm," she said, handing the dog over to him.

Ken closed the door and shook his finger at the dog. "You were bad."

Lucy bounded over. "A dog! I didn't know you had a dog."

The Rottweiler thumped his tail against the floor. It stood on all fours and looked Lucy in the eye, waggling its body side to side as it followed the happy tail.

Lucy hugged the dog enthusiastically. "What's its name?"

"Dog."

Edna sniffed disapproval. "Dog? What kind of a name is that?"

Ken shrugged. "He was given to me as a puppy a year ago, and I was so busy I never had time to think of a name. I just always called him Dog."

"Poor creature," Chris murmured, patting the sleek ebony coat. "Imagine if someone named you Human," she scolded Ken.

The slight curve at the corners of his mouth indicated his amusement at her concern. "Would you like to choose a better name? I don't think it's too late." He looked affectionately at the dog. "What do you think? Would you like a new name?"

Lucy looked at Ken with large round eyes. "Could we call him Bob? I always wanted a dog named Bob."

"I think Bob would be a great name for him. Why don't you take Bob into the kitchen and give him a breadstick while I talk to your mom a minute."

They both watched Lucy trot off with the dog. Chris felt Ken step closer to her. An electric flash ran along her spine and tingled at her fingertips. She felt his breath in her hair. "Uh"—she blinked in warm distress—"you wanted to talk to me?"

"Mmmm," he hummed in a raspy whisper, "but the words I want to say to you can't be said in front of Aunt Edna."

Without turning to look, Chris knew Aunt Edna had taken her position in the rocker and was keeping her eye on them. "Thank God for Aunt Edna." Chris laughed shakily.

He leaned away from her and assumed a more casual attitude. "If you don't have plans for the truck tonight, I'd like to make a trip out to Loudoun County. I'll leave Bob there. I think his style might be cramped in a townhouse. And I have to pick up some clothes."

"That would be fine. I don't have any lessons scheduled for tonight."

He whistled and called, "Bob!"

The dog bounded up to him. "He's so smart," he bragged. "You see how he knows his new name already?" He grabbed his vest from the hall coat rack, kissed Chris full on the lips, and swept out the door. Halfway down the sidewalk he turned. "I called your auto club and had them tow the car to a garage. The garage owner said he might be interested in buying it. Give him a call—the number's on the chalkboard."

Chris stood, rooted to the spot, as man and dog climbed into the truck and drove off. Lucy stood beside her, enthusiastically waving good-bye to Bob. When they reached the corner Chris closed her eyes tight in a sudden return to her senses.

"Oh, darn!" She smacked her fist against her forehead. She was going to kick him out after supper. Why did she let him go off to get his clothes?

Chris lay perfectly still under the patterns of silver moonlight that spilled through her bedroom window. The digital clock on her round, lace-covered night table read twelve forty-five. She was thinking about her marriage . . . about pain. She had blithely hurtled herself into a marriage that had brought her more pain and anger than she'd ever thought she could endure. But she'd managed to get through it. She had cried until there were no tears left in her body . . . for her unborn daughter who would never know her father . . . for her broken dream of sharing the joys of her pregnancy with the man she loved . . . for her terrible love for a man who really didn't exist. Her husband had been vain and shallow and ruthlessly ambitious— all gilt and no substance—and she had married him. She had fallen in love with falling in love. And it had taken years before her eyes were no longer clouded with being in love. Years before she'd been able to see the man for what he was and exorcise him from her life.

A tear slid down her cheek over the loss of what might have been. Another tear gathered in the fringe of her lower lashes. It was for the empty future, and for the ache of wanting to love Ken Callahan and knowing it would never be. She was not a good judge of men—that much was clear. She couldn't trust herself to fall in love again, because this time she wouldn't be the only one hurt. This time, when the love of her life turned out to be a rat, it would be Lucy's loss as well, and no one was going to hurt Lucy like that—not if she could help it. No one was going to blithely waltz into her daughter's life, and read her books, and get her to love him, and then leave.

She sat up in bed and scrubbed the tears from her eyes, piqued at this uncharacteristic bout with melancholia. It was all Ken Callahan's fault, barging into her life, with that unraveling grin and mouthwatering body, and stirring up feelings better left unstirred. She switched the table lamp on and immediately felt better as the room was bathed in a warm glow.

She'd decorated the room for the middle of the night. It was a room that could dispel the gloom and horror of the most terrible nightmare. It was a room that conjured up gentle sunshine and warm summer breezes. The light from the lamp reflected in the patina of her queen-sized brass bed. An ornate rolltop desk hugged one wall, it's pigeonholes overflowing with trinkets, dried flowers, bills, half-finished correspondence, and rolled-up magazines. It was framed by an assortment of pictures—pictures of trains, pictures of gorillas, pictures of ice skaters, pictures of family. The walls were the color of vanilla cream, the lush carpet a dusky rose, the down comforter covered by an apricot coverlet that matched an adjoining bath done entirely in apricot—including the walls and ceiling. Her brother had dubbed it her "sherbet phase," had merrily declared it to be sexist, and had concluded that his sister was substituting for all sorts of oral gratification.

"Probably," she'd told him breezily. "Who cares?" But deep down inside, she cared. She had made a terrible mistake, and she couldn't afford to make another. She couldn't afford the luxury of self-pity, and she couldn't admit to loneliness—not even to herself.

Pull yourself together, Chris, she fumed. Twelve forty-five. She had to be at the rink by five-twenty. She would be tired tomorrow, and it was all Ken's fault. He was sexy and charming—and a rogue. His first night under her roof, and he was off in Loudoun County, staying up to all hours and doing heaven-knows-what. It certainly didn't take five hours to gather a few clothes together. She threw the covers off and sprang out of bed. It was simple. She would go downstairs, she would make herself a cup of hot chocolate, and then she would go to sleep. And with any kind of luck, Ken Callahan would decide to stay in Loudoun County, and she'd never see him again.

She padded quietly downstairs and crept through the dark house. Reaching the kitchen, she switched on the light and set a pan of milk heating on the stove while she spooned the chocolate mix into a mug. The beginnings of a smile tipped the corners of her mouth. Her life was filled with small pleasures. Having a midnight treat in her cozy kitchen was one of them. She poured the milk into the mug and watched, enthralled, as the liquid became brown and steamy. It was her favorite mug—fine porcelain with a colorful picture of a mother rabbit. Her best friend Amy had given her a set of four because she knew Chris loved rabbits. There had been no special reason for the present—Amy had simply seen them, thought of Chris, and spent her last cent on the cups. And that was the whole point, Chris reasoned. She had Amy. She had Lucy. She had Aunt Edna. What did she need with Ken?

The cocoa cooled on the counter while Chris enjoyed the quiet. The refrigerator hummed as it defrosted. The sound of suburban traffic droned in the distance. A car door slammed. A key turned in her front door. Chris felt her heart skip a beat as the front door clicked open. It was him. Damn! What rotten luck—now she was trapped in the kitchen in her nightgown. She flicked the light switch, plunging the room into darkness. Maybe he hadn't seen the light. Maybe he wasn't hungry or thirsty. She closed her eyes in silent prayer. *Let him go directly to his room.*

A broad-shouldered, slim-hipped form appeared in the middle of the doorway. His face was bathed in shadow, giving Chris no clue to his mood. His good arm rested casually against the louvered door. "Hiding?" His voice was a velvet murmur. Low and purposefully seductive.

Rational thought and good intentions flew from her mind like autumn leaves on a windy day. She was aware only of the flame flickering to life deep within her. And she was suffused with the pleasure of his presence, with the predatory purr of his voice.

"You're standing in the moonlight, Chris. Would you like to know what I see?"

Chris felt her lips part, but no words emerged. She stood statue still, barely breathing, her heart thumping in her chest.

"I see a beautiful woman with silver curls and

moonbeams spilling over ivory shoulders and the curve of her arm. All highlight and shadow and breathless expectancy." He took a step toward her. "I'd be afraid to touch you if it weren't for the shadows."

"Shadows?"

He was very close now. Close enough for her to see his eyes, black with desire.

He drew the tip of his finger across her lower lip. "This shadow that tells me your lips are parted, waiting to be kissed." He closed his eyes, touched his mouth to hers, and he deepened the kiss. When she responded, he drew away to continue the seduction.

"And this shadow at your pulse point," he murmured, his lips across her neck.

She closed her eyes and moaned softly, succumbing to the pleasure that ripped through her body at his every touch, wanting to feel him against her. Again, Chris was treated to a searing flash of foresight, a reaffirming of what she'd sensed in the hospital: that Ken would be a careful, sensitive lover; that he would allow their desire to build until it was unbearable; and that when his passion was finally unleashed, it would be all-encompassing, devastatingly intense, and like none she had ever known.

His mouth found hers with startling urgency. Chris leaned into him. Her breasts pressed against his muscled chest. She kissed him without reserve.

"I need you." He kissed her again, long and deep. "I need you to love me." He swung around to lift her in his arms, forgetting the day-old cast. *C-l-a-n-n-n-g!* The plaster cast smashed against an empty copper fruit bowl sitting innocently on the counter. The bowl sailed through space and clattered onto the floor. *Arrrrang arrrrang arrrrang!* The bowl whirled to a stop.

"Oh my God!" Chris choked.

"What the hell was that?"

Chris choked back laughter and bent to retrieve the bowl. "It was a copper bowl."

Lights flashed on upstairs. A door was thrown open. "What's going on down there?" Edna yelled.

They looked at each other like two children caught pilfering the cookie jar.

Ken rested his forehead against a cabinet door. "I think I might cry."

"I think I might buy more fruit bowls."

"Saved by the bell, huh?"

Chris looked at him in the moonlight. His face was still tinged with the strain of unsated desire. "I didn't mean for this to happen," she explained in a voice that was shaky with emotion. "I couldn't sleep, and I was making myself a cup of cocoa."

"I guessed. I could smell the cocoa as soon as I opened the front door." He took the fruit bowl from her and set it back on the counter. "And I didn't mean for *this* to happen," he told her with a menacing grin aimed at the now-silent bowl.

"Yeah," Chris breathed. "I believe that."

Aunt Edna's voice rattled down the stairs. "Chris? Is that you making that racket?"

"Yes, Aunt Edna. I was making cocoa, and I accidentally knocked the fruit bowl off the counter."

"Land sakes," she grumbled, "scared the daylights out of me."

"Why don't you come down and have some cocoa with me?"

Ken shook his finger at her. "Shame on you. That's so cowardly."

"And so wise."

"A cup of cocoa," Edna repeated happily. "Don't that sound nice! I'll go get my robe."

Ken reluctantly pushed himself away from Chris. "You'll regret this as much as I will. You'll lie in bed for the rest of the evening feeling unsatisfied and wanting me, and I won't be able to come to you."

Chris shivered at the sexy timbre of his voice and the lethal calm in his eyes. She knew he was right, but she had no choice. *Thank goodness for Aunt Edna. I have no defenses against this man. I feel like a moth being drawn into the flame.*

Aunt Edna's slippered feet slapped against the stair carpet.

Ken turned and left before Edna reached the kitchen.

Chris wrapped her arms across her breasts and was consumed with an all-encompassing loneliness for Ken Callahan.

Chapter 4

Chris looked at the slim gold watch on her wrist and groaned. Five-ten. She was late. She was tired. She was cranky. And she certainly didn't have time for breakfast. She slung the gray sports bag over her shoulder and shuffled down the dark stairs. Ordinarily, Aunt Edna would be up making breakfast, but she'd overslept today, too. Chris shrugged into her vest and reached for the doorknob.

A large hand closed over her small one. "Making a hasty retreat?"

Chris turned and found herself squashed between the door and Ken. He smiled good morning and kissed her softly, as if she were a delicate treasure. He was right, she thought, he was a terrific kisser. She halfheartedly reminded herself that she was grouchy and didn't want to be kissed . . . or talked to . . . or smiled at. She tried to look stern. "What are you doing up so early?"

"I want to watch you teach ice skating."

Chris wrinkled her nose. "It's five-ten. It's dark out. The birds aren't even up yet. Go back to bed."

"Are you kidding? I even took a shower to do this."

"Well, I don't feel like having an audience today. I'm tired and grumpy . . . and I don't want to be bothered by you."

"Hmmmm, couldn't you sleep last night?" His tone was mockingly innocent and maddeningly triumphant.

She tilted her nose up defiantly. "I slept fine after I had my cocoa."

"I'm glad cocoa has such a soothing effect on you." He nuzzled her hair, inhaling the scent of her shampoo. "I didn't have any cocoa to soothe my frustration. I lay awake all night, thinking about you."

Chris wound her arms around his neck and murmured in contentment. "Poor Ken."

He chuckled softly and kissed her neck. "You're so responsive. So nice to love."

And dumb. And weak. And sappy. Had that been her voice murmuring "Poor Ken"? "Ugh! Get away from me." Chris pushed him away, stamping her foot in frustration. "What is it about you that turns me into mush?"

Ken sucked in his breath as her boot accidentally came down on his bare foot. He stood absolutely still for a second, his right hand holding her arm in a viselike grip. He expelled his breath and closed his eyes. The expletive that escaped between his clenched teeth caused Chris to raise her eyebrows.

"You'd better not let Aunt Edna hear you say that. She'll let you have it with the wooden spoon."

He relaxed his hand, smoothed the fingerprints from the sleeve of her warm-up suit, and regarded her with calm fury. "You broke my toe."

Chris looked down at the bloody gash and already swelling toe. "Why don't you have shoes on?" she wailed.

"Because I can't get shoes on by myself. Because you broke my damn arm. Because I haven't had a chance to buy loafers, yet."

Chris bit her lip. "Maybe it's not broken?"

"I'm sure it's broken. I'm getting good at recognizing broken bones."

"Maybe we should put some ice on it."

"I don't want ice," he ground out. "I want to go to the hospital." He lowered himself gingerly onto a stair and held out a sock. "Just help me put this damn sock on . . . and this damn shoe. And then you can drive me to the damn hospital."

Chris glared at him and tugged the sock onto his healthy foot. She slipped his running shoe on and tied the laces. "I don't see what you're so damn mad about. It isn't as if it's entirely my fault."

"Not entirely your fault?" he sputtered. "Lady, you're a fruitcake. I suppose you think I saw your boot coming down, and I slipped my toe underneath it on purpose."

"You know perfectly well what I mean. You . . . you take advantage of me."

"Well, you're not going to have to worry about it anymore. I can't afford to break any more body parts. At this rate, I'll be a paraplegic by Friday. And God forbid what might happen if I ever got you into bed! A man would have to be crazy to take his clothes off anywhere near you."

Chris grit her teeth and held his other sock out to him. "Do you want me to put this on you?"

"Don't touch my foot!" he shouted. "Just get me a towel so I don't bleed all over my truck."

By the time she returned with the towel, he'd already hobbled out to the curb.

Chris stopped for a light and nervously cracked her knuckles. It had been a long, silent ride to the hospital. Ken slouched in the seat next to her, staring stonily straight ahead, his arms crossed in front of him. He hadn't said a word since they'd left the house, and Chris was afraid to begin conversation. What on earth do you say to a man after you've broken his toe? And his arm. Glorioski, Mr. Callahan, I'm really sorry! Chris felt tears burning behind her eyes. *Thank goodness for the darkness*, she breathed. *This is awful enough, I don't need to have him see me crying. I don't even know why I'm feeling such anguish over this whole silly episode.* She blinked back the tears and decided it must be hormones. The man was hell on hormones.

She heard him rustle in the seat beside her, and knew with a sinking heart that he was watching her. His fingertips brushed across her cheek.

"What's this for?"

Chris ignored the question. She turned into the hospital lot and cut the motor. "Would you rather I come in with you? Or should I wait here?"

"I'd rather you tell me why you're crying."

Chris stared miserably down at her warm-up jacket.

He reached over with his good arm and hauled her across the seat, onto his lap.

"Be careful! Your arm! Your toe!"

He kissed the tears on her cheek and nestled her into the crook of his arm. "Honey, when I've got you on my lap I can't even feel my arm or my toe."

Chris closed her eyes and buried her flushed face into his shoulder.

His lips feathered lingering kisses in her orange curls. "You like me, don't you?" he said in a husky whisper that sent her heart tumbling in her chest.

She couldn't speak. She was overwhelmed with a rush of conflicting emotions. She did like him. Even more horrible, she might be falling in love with him. How else to explain the lump that was becoming a permanent fixture in her throat? How else to explain the sense of dread—of impending doom—of unwanted, fingertip-tingling excitement? She nodded her head yes, and pressed her cheek against his chest.

"And you're sorry you broke my toe?"

She nodded again.

"Is there anything else?"

Chris sighed. There were about a million other things, but none she wanted to say out loud. And nothing she could coherently explain when he was kissing her hair. Warm waves of desire were washing away sensible thought. She concluded that if she stayed in his arms for another thirty seconds she would lose all control and attack him, and they'd probably be arrested for doing X-rated things in a hospital parking lot. She took a deep breath and pushed herself from his lap. "I suppose I do like you, a little," Chris admitted. "And I'm sorry about your toe, but I think we should keep this living arrangement strictly business."

"Why?"

Chris squeezed her finely arched eyebrows together into a frown. "Because I'm not too happy about having a man in my house. And I definitely don't want one in my life. I like my life just the way it is . . . was . . . before yesterday."

He regarded her with open amusement. "What a load of baloney."

"Unh!" she grunted. "You are the most exasperating man." She threw her hands into the air in frustration. "Go get your blasted toe fixed."

Ken looked at the stretch of cold macadam between the truck and the reception room. He looked down at his blue-and-purple bare foot partially wrapped in an apricot hand towel.

"Sorry," she whispered. "I wasn't thinking." She started the truck and drove to the emergency entrance where he got out and hobbled inside.

Chris parked and joined him at the front desk, where he was filling out a form. An inquisitive nurse leaned over the desk and looked at his toe. "Weren't you folks in here yesterday?"

Ken raised his bright green cast. "Yesterday she broke my arm," he announced merrily.

A second nurse appeared. Chris felt her face flame as the two nurses studied her suspiciously.

Ken completed the form. He raised his foot. "Today she broke my toe."

"It was an accident," Chris gasped.

The nurses looked at each other knowingly and studiously returned to their work.

"How could you embarrass me like that?" Chris looked around furtively to see if anyone else had heard.

"It's okay." He grinned. "She probably thought it was part of some bizarre sexual ritual."

"Good heavens."

"You should probably call the rink now and tell them you'll be late, again."

Chris stared at Ken, struck by the unpleasant reality that she'd sent this man to the hospital two days in a row—and that if positions had been reversed, she doubted she could be so good-natured. "I suppose I should be happy you have a sense of humor," she ventured.

"Honey, my good mood has little to do with my sense of humor."

Aunt Edna's eyes opened wide as she stood back from the door. "What the devil happened?"

Ken carefully swung his foot over the door-jamb and eased himself into the room with the help of a single crutch. "It's nothing serious, Aunt Edna. I stubbed my toe in the dark this morning and broke it."

Chris slammed the door behind them. "He did not. He got fresh with me, and I stomped on it."

Ken rested on his crutch, and looked at her quizzically. "I thought you found that story embarrassing."

"Oh, what the hell," she exclaimed in an off-hand huff. "So I broke it. What's the big deal?"

Ken smiled at Aunt Edna. "She's sorry she broke it."

Edna looked at the swollen toe taped to the one next to it. "He got fresh with you, huh?"

"Yes. Well, no. He sort of got me . . . disturbed."

"Hmmm," Edna said. "Disturbed?"

Ken slouched into the wingback chair and stretched his long legs in front of him, watching Chris with unguarded affection. "Disturbed?" he asked, the twitching corners of his mouth the only evidence of strangled laughter.

"I'd love to stay and explain all of this," Chris told them, "but I've got to get to the rink."

"Will you be home for lunch?" Edna asked.

Chris kissed the old woman good-bye and headed for the door. "No, I have to do some choreography today. I probably won't be back until suppertime."

Chris checked her watch as she walked up the steps to her town house. It was six-fifteen, and she felt as if she hadn't slept in days. She opened the door and sniffed. A delicious aroma of herbs and spices wafted through the house. Aunt Edna's world-famous oven-fried chicken, she decided. She flung her bag into a corner of the hall and shuffled toward the kitchen. It was after a terribly long day like this that she was especially thankful for Aunt Edna. If it weren't for Edna, Chris knew she'd be staring into the freezer right now, wondering what the heck she could shove into the microwave. If it weren't for Edna, the role of breadwinner and single mother would leave little time for Chris to read Dr. Seuss or listen attentively to Lucy's exploits in school. Chris pushed through the kitchen doors. "Aunt Edna—"

Ken turned from the stove and gave her a look like the cat who swallowed the canary. "Nope. Just me, slaving away over a hot stove."

"Where's Aunt Edna?"

"Kansas City."

"What do you mean, Kansas City?"

"Your cousin Stephanie had the baby three weeks premature and Edna flew out to stay with the twins."

"How could she do that?"

"Stephanie? I don't think she had much choice. George said her water broke at three twenty-five and she went right into labor . . ."

Chris blinked in dazed disbelief. Yesterday he'd been a stranger. Today he was ensconced in her kitchen, talking about her family as if it were his own. Babies and labor and broken water. "No," she intoned mechanically, "not Stephanie . . . Aunt Edna. How could Aunt Edna do this to me? It will take me days to find someone reliable to watch Lucy."

"Edna took Lucy with her."

"She can't do that! What about school?"

Ken took a bag of noodles from the counter and looked at it, mystified. He turned the bag over and read the instructions, his face brightening with the realization that he now knew how to cook noodles. "Edna said she'll only be gone for a week, and that Lucy could use a vacation. I don't think Edna is very impressed with first grade."

Cold panic squeezed at Chris' heart. The two people she loved most in the world were gone without even so much as a hug good-bye. And she was left alone with Ken Callahan. It was the latter condition that set her stomach churning and adrenaline flowing.

Ken reached out and gathered her to him. "You look like a lost little kitten," he said. He stroked her hair. "Don't worry. They'll be fine. I took them to the airport myself. And Edna said they'd call as soon as they got to Kansas City."

"How did you get them to the airport?"

"Taxi." He raised his foot to display a bright red woolen sock covering the broken toe. "A broken toe isn't so bad."

She stepped away from him. "It was nice of you to help Edna and Lucy to the airport, but you're going to have to leave, now."

"I live here, remember?"

"I don't want you to live here."

Ken filled a pot with water and put it on the stove to boil. "Of course you do. Who will make your supper when you come home late like this?"

"You?" she snorted.

He pulled a package of frozen vegetables from the freezer and read the instructions. "I always wanted to learn how to cook." He set the vegetables aside and dumped the entire bag of noodles into the boiling water.

"Holy cow," Chris muttered. "I hope you like noodles. That could feed a family of six for two days."

He seemed undaunted. "Hmmm," he replied and emptied sixteen ounces of peas into a small saucepan. He smiled at her. "I surmise by the look of horror on your face that I'm cooking too many peas too."

"I usually measure out about half and then tie the rest of the bag up with a twister tie."

"Twister tie?"

Chris wrinkled her nose. "This isn't going to work. I don't need a cook. I think your aptitude is dubious, anyway."

"Boy, you get cranky after a hard day at the skating rink," he teased. He pushed her into the dining room and held her chair.

Chris looked at the table. Matching mauve linen tablecloth and napkins. Crystal goblets. The good china. Sterling candlestick holders and ivory tapers. Freshly polished silverware. "You've gone to a lot of trouble. It's very pretty."

"Actually, Aunt Edna did it. She wanted me to make a good impression on you."

"Hmmm."

"She likes me."

"She's not too choosy, you realize. Last week

she fixed me up with the meter reader. And before that it was the butcher."

"Why is she so determined to get you married?"

"I suppose because she had a wonderful marriage, and she wants the same for me."

Ken leaned against the table and studied Chris. "Wouldn't you like a wonderful marriage?"

"I've already tried marriage. It wasn't wonderful."

"But it could be. Don't you want to give it another shot?"

"No."

"Edna told me you were a great skater because you never gave up."

"I never gave up on skating because I knew I was good. I'm not good at being married." Chris turned away from the intensity of his blue-black gaze. Why was he doing this—it wasn't like he was ready to propose or something.

"I think you'd make a great wife. You just need some practice."

"Uh-huh." Chris turned back toward him, one eyebrow raised quizzically.

"I could help you out . . ." He grinned. "You could practice on me."

"That's a very generous offer, but I think I'll pass." The sound of sputtering water turning to steam hissed from the kitchen. "The peas"—Chris gestured—"turn down the heat."

A lid clanked in the kitchen. Silence followed. "Okay," he finally called, "I give up. How the hell do you get these peas out of all this water?"

Endearing, Chris thought. Ruggedly masculine but soft on the underside. And very skillful at using his devastating smile and easy humor. She took the copper colander from the kitchen wall and placed it in the sink. "You can pour the peas in here. And then you can use the colander to drain and rinse the noodles."

He gave a light husbandly kiss. "Thanks. Any other cooking tips I should know?"

"Are you really serious about this?"

"Absolutely." He put the peas in the glass bowl Edna had left on the counter for him. He poured the steaming noodles into the colander and ran water over them. "How am I doing?"

Chris gave him a begrudging smile. He was doing fine with the noodles, and he was doing fine with his assignment of making a good impression. Ken was a man who knew how to drop back and punt. They carried the food into the dining room and took places opposite each other.

Ken looked at Edna's chicken with reverent admiration.

"I'm not sure I've ever seen a man look at a piece of chicken like that."

"I can't remember the last time I had home cooking. It seems like I've been on the road for a century." He put a pat of butter on his noodles and watched it melt. "My mother is a great cook—she makes these noodles in a cheese sauce . . ." He looked up at her with beguiling blue eyes. "Do you know how to do that? Do you suppose you could teach me to make cheese sauce?"

"There's a recipe for cheese sauce in the recipe box on the counter." She studied him intently for a minute, trying to imagine Ken as a young boy. He'd probably been spoiled rotten. What mother could say no to those big blue eyes? "Tell me about your family."

He sliced a piece of chicken and chewed it thoughtfully. "I guess I come from a large family by today's standards—one brother and three sisters. I'm the oldest, and I'm the only one unmarried. My parents still live in the same two-story frame house that I grew up in—in Pennsylvania. Nothing fancy, but lots of love and lots of noise. I have six nephews and four nieces. You can't imagine what Christmas Day sounds like."

"Does everyone come to your parents' house for Christmas?"

Ken speared another piece of chicken. "The kids enjoy getting their presents under their own Christmas trees." He savored a forkful of buttered noodles and grinned. "They were afraid Santa wouldn't know to bring their presents to my parents' house, so we designated December twenty-eighth as Family Christmas every year. It makes it easier to travel, too. My brother lives in Connecticut. My sister Maggie moved to Seattle last year. Cara lives in Cape May. My youngest sister, Erin, is the only one still in Pennsylvania. She lives about a half mile from my parents."

"Sounds like a nice family."

Ken nodded. "I don't get to see them as much as I'd like." He looked critically at the bowl still filled with peas. "Too many peas," he agreed, taking another helping. "What about you? Do your parents still live in Colorado?"

Chris shook her head. "My mom died when I was nineteen. My dad died three years ago. Heart disease."

"I'm sorry."

Chris nodded.

"You have a brother?"

"Ted. Two years older than me. He's still in Colorado." Her gaze rested on his competent hands, slicing off another bite of chicken.

"What brought you east?"

"This job," she said, turning her attention back to her own plate. "They needed someone with international experience to build a competitive skate program. It's a small rink, but it has some good skaters—last year two of my students qualified for national competition."

"You like teaching skating." He speared a final forkful of noodles.

"I love it. I find it much more satisfying than competing. And much less painful."

Ken looked at his empty plate with a contented sigh. "And I find cooking much more satisfying than construction work."

Chris laughed softly. "What you find satisfying is eating . . . not cooking."

He raised his eyes, suddenly filled with a hunger that had nothing to do with peas or oven-fried chicken. "I have something special planned for dessert."

Chris felt her temperature rise and wondered how he did it. With a single teasing sentence and one semismoldering look, he had instantly turned her into a quivering mass of overheated half-wit. She narrowed her eyes and hoped she looked menacing. "You looking to get something else broken?"

Ken raised his hands in mock self-defense. His

eyes softened with the recognition of her panic. "You don't like dessert?" he asked in exaggerated innocence.

She shook her finger at him. "You weren't talking about dessert."

He began stacking the dishes. "I was going to suggest Irish coffee in front of a roaring fire, and"—he disappeared behind the kitchen door—"a plate full of goodies." He reappeared with a bakery bag and a sterling plate covered with a paper doily. "I stopped at a bakery on the way home from the airport. You fix the cookies, and I'll make coffee. I may not be much of a cook, but I make an excellent Irish coffee."

Chris stared at the white bag. It was from her favorite bakery. She peeked inside. All her favorite cookies—and Linzer tortes. She loved Linzer tortes. Smells like a plot, she thought. This could only be Aunt Edna's work. The heavenly aroma of coffee brewing drifted into the dining room. Chris sniffed in appreciation and arranged the cookies on the silver plate. A doily. She sighed. Edna was really going all out on this one.

"Chris," Ken called. "I need help. I can't carry two mugs of hot coffee with only one hand."

Chris placed the cookies and the coffee on a tray and followed Ken downstairs. There was already a fire glowing in the fireplace. An electric thrill raced through Chris as she watched Ken add a log and stoke the embers into life. He wore a powder-blue polo shirt with the left sleeve cut at the elbow. His silky black hair curled over the cotton collar, the muscles in his back rippled as he moved, and his biceps bulged under the soft fabric. Chris allowed herself the intoxicating pleasure of admiring the broad shoulders and slim hips. His shirt hung loose over clean, faded jeans that were loose enough to be comfortable, but tight enough to display well-defined quadriceps and a perfect backside. *I'd trade every Linzer torte on this plate for one nibble at that perfect behind*, she decided, and was immediately horrified that she'd even thought such a thing. She felt her face flame.

He rose from the fire and regarded her with amused curiosity. "Are you flushed from the fire, or have you been thinking naughty thoughts?"

Chris put her hands to her burning cheeks. "This is embarrassing."

He settled beside her on the big overstuffed couch and rested his injured foot on the coffee table. "Here"—he offered Chris half of his sugar cookie—"take a bite. It will be so exquisite you'll forget about being embarrassed."

Chris bit into the cookie and let it melt in her

mouth, ruefully thinking it would take more than a cookie to overcome her undeniable reaction to his presence. Sexy. She tried taking slow, deep, regular breaths, but her heart was still pounding.

"Edna told me about this bakery. She said it was your favorite—I can see why." He waved his half-eaten piece of cookie at her. "I'm an expert on cookies, and these are definitely top of the line."

Chris licked at the dollop of whipped cream floating on the top of her coffee. His honesty was unnerving. He made no pretense about Edna's help in all this, and he made it perfectly clear that he was on his best behavior, trying to make a good impression. Chris wondered about his intentions. He obviously wanted to live in her house. She wasn't sure why, except that he really did seem to miss being part of a family. And he was physically attracted to her. That was unmistakable. And mutual. No man had ever affected her quite like Ken— not even Steven.

Chris watched him under lowered lashes and felt the warmth flood through her. It was a bittersweet feeling, lovely and sensual as a cat by a heated hearth, and sad because it was all so impossible. *I don't want another man in my life*, she repeated to herself. *Especially this one. He's much too handsome. Too virile. He probably collects women like ants at a picnic.* But she had to admit this was very nice.

They sat side by side on the comfortable couch, eating Linzer tortes in silence, listening to the hiss and crackle of the fire. Chris sipped at the coffee. She curled her legs under her and closed her eyes drowsily. "It's been such a long day," she mumbled in halfhearted apology. "I can't keep my eyes open."

Chapter 5

"Come on, sleepyhead." Ken's voice was as gentle as the hand that stroked her cheek. "Time to get up."

Chris blinked in the darkness, trying to organize the confusion of her mind.

Ken smiled at her. It was an irresistible, devastating grin—even at the crack of dawn. His white teeth flashed in his black beard, reminding Chris of a pirate. "You fell asleep right in the middle of your Linzer torte last night," he said with a trace of laughter. "You mumbled something about it being a long day and then you were gone."

"Did Edna call?"

"Yes. Everyone is fine. You should call Kansas later this morning. Lucy lost a tooth somewhere over Wheeling, West Virginia. I think she'd like to brag to you about it."

A shaft of golden light escaped from his open bedroom door, partially illuminating the rec room.

Chris gazed sleepily at the man sitting beside her. She unconsciously reached out and touched a lock of black hair that was still wet from his shower. "You smell nice. Warm and spicy . . . like men's soap and mint toothpaste."

He captured her hand and pressed a lingering kiss against the inside of her wrist. His eyes held her. "Be careful. It wouldn't take much to get me under that quilt with you."

Chris felt her heart jump at the touch of his lips. *It wouldn't take much for me to drag you under here,* she silently groaned. "I . . . uh . . . I was just . . ." She closed her eyes tight. "Oh damn. You've got me stuttering."

"Mmmm, I seem to have a strange effect on you."

"Yeah. An annoying mixture of lust and sheer panic, and I intend to ignore both of them." She stretched under the down quilt. "I see you tucked me in."

"I considered undressing you and putting you to bed, but I didn't want to risk another broken body part. I need all the parts I have left."

"Very wise." She sat up and rubbed her eyes. "What time is it?"

"Four-thirty. Better get moving. Breakfast will be served in twenty minutes."

She looked at him warily. "Are you cooking breakfast?"

"Edna told me you have orange juice, coffee, and an egg over easy."

Chris shook her head and muttered to herself as she climbed the stairs. "The woman even told him what I have for breakfast. Heaven only knows what else she told him. He probably knows my shoe size and my cholesterol level."

Chris locked her bedroom door and her bathroom door and still felt uncomfortable when she stripped for her shower. There was no escaping Ken. He had invaded her bastion of female tranquility and security. He permeated every part of the house. He stirred every latent sex-related hormone in her body.

She lathered her shoulders and watched the soap cascade in slippery rivulets. She was suddenly glad she had kept herself in shape. Thank goodness I inherited a healthy metabolism and a naturally slim body from my mother, she thought. Her hectic schedule didn't leave time for fancy spas and tennis dates. She exercised daily with the skaters in a general conditioning class and tried to run at least six miles a week. She examined herself more closely. Her waist was still small and supple. Her stomach was flat. Her legs still showed good muscle definition in the quadriceps and calves. Not an ounce of fat, she concluded with great satisfaction. She ducked her head under the steaming water and poured shampoo into the tangle of orange curls.

Of course, she assured herself, the fact that she was taking an appraisal of her body for the first time in seven years had nothing to do with Ken Callahan. She simply had a little extra time this morning and had happened to notice she was still trim and desirable. In fact, she had so much time she decided to use the expensive herbal rinse that made her hair shiny and soft to touch. She whisked out of the shower, humming happily, towel-dried her hair, and smoothed moisturizer over her flawless complexion.

The warm-up suits neatly folded in her dresser drawer seemed strangely bland. They were comfortable and sensible . . . and blah. Mostly gray. Not today, she decided. She didn't feel gray. She felt red. Maybe turquoise. And she didn't feel a bit baggy. She rummaged through her bottom drawer, finally finding a black Lycra skintight body suit with stirrup feet. She ripped the tags off a brand-new, sparkling-white turtleneck and pulled it over her head and added a black sweater with bright blue-and-white racing stripes running the length of the arm. A quick look in the mirror brought a smile to her lips as she settled the wide ribbing on her hips. She carefully added a touch of shadow, swiped at her lashes with the mascara wand, and was startled to find that her cheeks were glowing pink without blusher. "Must have been the hot shower," she said, putting her makeup brush down.

Chris flew down the stairs and pushed through the kitchen door. A pregnant silence filled the small room. There was a peculiar expression on Ken's face as he stood by the stove. He seemed poised on the brink of some emotion—a look of general horror about him; his eyes wide with surprise, his mouth twitching with what might be laughter, his black brows drawn together in consternation. Chris stopped still in her tracks. She followed his eyes to a spot on the floor just inches from her feet. Her first reaction was to classify the object on the floor with snakes, spiders, mice, and unidentified slime. She jumped back a foot and screamed. "Eeeeeh! What is it?" When it didn't move she bent down to take a closer look and realized it was an egg. Perfectly fried. Over easy.

"It's an egg," he said tonelessly. "Over easy. Just the way you like it."

"You did a good job," Chris told him, almost

choking. "It's perfect. Except . . ."—she swallowed hard—"except it's on the floor."

"The little devil slid out of the pan."

Chris clapped her hands over her mouth in an attempt to abort the gales of laughter that were rising in her throat.

Ken bent over the egg with her. "You may as well go ahead and laugh. You look like you're ready to burst an eardrum from internal pressure."

"I'm sorry," she gasped between spasms of hysteria. "I really am sorry."

"It's the first egg I've ever cooked . . . in my entire life." He slid the spatula under the egg and lifted it from the linoleum. "I think it's dead."

Chris stood ramrod straight, saluted the egg, and tooted out taps.

Ken gave her a withering look and dumped the mess into the garbage disposal. "Would you like me to try again?"

"No. I think I'll pass on the egg today." She swallowed her juice and sipped at the coffee. "Mmmm. You do make excellent coffee."

Ken lounged against the wall, watching her with an intensity that made her feel as if she were melting inch by inch. Slowly and hungrily, his eyes traveled the length of her. "Do you have any idea what you look like? Does Aunt Edna let you go out dressed like that?"

Chris bit back a smile. Damn right she knew what she looked like—sexy as all get-out. And Edna would do cartwheels to get her to dress like this. Edna hated the warm-up suits. Edna called them camouflage.

Chris feigned innocence. "What's wrong with this?"

"It's . . . slinky." His face clouded. "Beautiful soft orange curls and eyes like a young lioness . . . and now this outfit." He reached out and ran his finger along the outside of her thigh. "It's silky," he noted, molding his hand to her hipbone. "It fits you like skin. What on earth is this? Something special for skaters?"

"It's a body suit."

He peeked under her sweater with more curiosity than passion. "It goes all the way up."

Chris slapped at his hand. "Don't do that!"

He smoothed the ribbing back over her hips. His eyes softened until Chris thought he looked like a blue-eyed cocker spaniel. "You're such an enigma, Chris Nelson. Flushed cheeks and soft lips and a little breathless. When you direct all that wide-eyed excitement at me it turns my stomach upside down." He cupped her chin in his hand and rubbed his thumb lightly across her lower lip. "I've fallen in love with you, and I'm worried because you're sending me such a mixture of signals. Sometimes I think you're beginning to like me, and then all of a sudden panic sets in and you get all bristly."

Fallen in love with her! Chris felt as if someone were squeezing the air from her lungs. "I don't want you to fall in love with me," she gasped. "And I certainly don't want to fall in love with you."

"What's wrong with me?"

Chris found herself smiling at his injured tone. "Nothing's wrong with you. That's the problem . . . you're perfect. You're attractive and sensitive and fun to be with. I could easily fall in love with you . . . if I wanted to fall in love."

Ken plunged his hands into his pockets and studied her. "You don't want to fall in love?"

Chris turned away from him and nervously smoothed an imaginary wrinkle in her sweater. Of course she wanted to fall in love. Everyone wanted to fall in love. Real love must be wonderful. But fake love is awful . . . and she obviously wasn't capable of telling the difference. She'd thought Steven had loved her. What a laugh. She folded her hands in front of her to keep from fiddling with the sweater. "I can't fall in love," she told him quietly.

"Why not?"

"It's too painful." She heard her voice falter and took a deep breath to pull herself together. "I have a very nice life. I don't have any intention of complicating it with an emotionally draining relationship."

Ken crossed his arms over his chest and studied her. "I can understand how you feel. You've had a terrible experience, and you're afraid to let yourself love again. But it's wrong for you to judge me by the asinine behavior of another man."

Chris turned and faced him. "Right or wrong has nothing to do with it. It's simply survival and motherly instincts and my own personal limitations. I'm not ready to open myself up that much to someone again. I may never be ready."

Chris lowered her eyes and inspected her shoe. The ensuing silence seemed thick with tension and bitter thoughts. Finally Ken cleared his throat, and she looked up.

His eyes sparkled with mischief. "So, you don't want to get married, and you don't want to fall in love. How do you feel about casual sex?"

Chris felt a grudging smile tug at the corners of her mouth. "I don't do casual sex."

Ken slid his hand to her waist and drew her to him, burying his face in her curly hair. His lips were warm, and soft and coaxing. His tongue teased lightly over hers. She felt him savor the kiss as if it were a forbidden and rare delicacy, and her heart responded to the compliment with an aching desire for more. They parted slowly, watching each other dreamily, delighting in the sensual intimacy that lingered. Chris felt him withdraw. A look of questioning uncertainty flickered in his blue eyes for just a moment and was replaced with resolute calmness. Then he sighed and held her at arm's length. "If you don't want to fall in love, and you don't want to have meaningless sex . . . what the hell is this that's happening between us?"

Chris bit her lower lip. "It's a total lack of will-power. There's something about you that turns me into mindless overheated mush."

"Mindless overheated mush? Is that anything like gruel? Or Quaker Oats?"

Chris threw her hands into the air. "It isn't funny. I hate it—and it's all your fault. No one else has ever done this to me; you have some horrible effect on my hormones."

His eyes opened wide in pleased surprise. A smile twitched over his mouth. "Really?" he said, gloating. "How terrible!"

Chris observed his unabashed glee with embarrassed fury. "And you should be ashamed of yourself. Here you are taking advantage of my . . . affliction."

He grinned at her in silent amazement. "Affliction? If I thought you were serious I'd really be mad."

"I am serious," she snapped, more out of momentum than seriousness.

He held the curve of her jaw in his hand. "You're a healthy, sensuous, responsive woman. That's a beautiful gift, not an affliction. And you're wrong about my taking advantage of the situation. I don't want you doing something you'll regret just because I stir up your hormones." He tapped her temple with his index finger. "When I take you to bed it will be all of you. Your lovely illogical mind included." He spun her around and pushed her toward the front door. "We'll talk about this more over dinner. If you don't hurry, you'll be late for work."

Chris checked her watch and grimaced—she had no time in her schedule for knee-weakening kisses or men falling in love.

Ken reached into the hall closet and extracted Chris' ski jacket. "It's supposed to be cold today— maybe some snow," he told Chris, zipping her into the coat as if she were going off to kindergarten. "Be careful driving home." He gave her a slow, lingering kiss and playfully swatted her behind as she swung through the door.

She turned with an indignant profanity on the tip of her tongue, decided that a simple pat on the backside didn't warrant that much hostility, pressed her lips together in fury, and hurried to the truck. After all, she admitted, she was mad at Chris Nelson, not Ken Callahan. Ken Callahan hadn't actually done anything wrong . . . darn it.

Bitsy leaned against the rink guardrail and smiled at Chris. "You look like you have a lot on your mind."

"Mmmmmm."

"I can't tell if you're depressed or elated. You have the most peculiar expression on your face."

"Then it registers my mood perfectly."

"A man?"

"Mmmmmm."

A devilish grin spread across Bitsy's face. "The man in the truck?"

"Yeah," Chris sighed. "Did I tell you he's living with me?"

Bitsy's eyes widened. "Fast work!"

Chris wrinkled her nose. "No. It's nothing like

that. Well, it is sort of . . . oh hell! Aunt Edna rented him the downstairs of the house."

Bitsy tipped her head back and bellowed out a laugh. "Good old Aunt Edna. Somehow, I'm not surprised."

"That's not even the worst of it. My cousin Stephanie went into labor yesterday, and Edna flew off to Kansas City to help out with the twins. And she took Lucy with her."

Bitsy looked more interested by the second. "So it's just the two of you in the house?" She giggled.

"You can stop thinking whatever you're thinking. Nothing happened."

"You sound disappointed."

Chris slouched against the barrier. "I don't know. He's really yummy, but I've finally gotten over that stinker, Steven. I don't want to let another man into my life. My life is calm and orderly, now. It's comfortable." Chris screwed up her face for emphasis. "It's been over seven years since I've been really intimate with a man, and I haven't missed it . . . until Ken arrived on the scene. Now it's like an obsession. An enormous all-consuming blot on my life. Three days ago I didn't know this man existed, and now he's all I think about. I can't get near him without coming unglued. I do everything but drool." She touched her hands to her cheek. "Look at me. I get hot flashes just thinking about him."

"Wow."

"And if that isn't bad enough . . . I even like him."

Bitsy looked horrified. "I think you've slipped a cog somewhere."

"My cogs are fine." Chris bent to adjust one of her skate laces, then straightened with a sigh. "I just don't want to complicate my life. I have my work and Lucy and Edna; I don't have the time or the energy for a love affair. And I'm a terrible judge of men—what if he turns out to be another Steven Black?"

Bitsy fixed her with a direct, steady gaze. "There's only one Steven Black."

It was true, Chris admitted as she parked the truck in front of her town house that evening. There was only one Steven Black, and it wasn't fair to judge Ken by Steven's failings. She sat for a moment watching the promised snow sift down in giant flakes and melt on the hood of the truck. It clung tentatively to the already frozen lawn and cement sidewalk. The front porch light had been turned on to welcome her home, and soft lights glowed behind the drawn living room curtains. A small thrill of happiness fluttered through her stomach at the cozy scene. Her armor was definitely slipping. She'd do better to overlook the homey welcome and conjure images of virile spiders waiting for naive flies instead . . .

The sharp whine of a siren pierced the stillness, and Chris quirked an eyebrow. The smoke detector! She bolted to her front door and flung it open, only to be met by a cloud of gray smoke that stung her eyes and choked in her throat. "Ken!"

"I'm in the damn kitchen," he shouted over the din of the smoke detector.

"Are you okay? Should I call the fire department?"

"I can't figure out how to get this blasted alarm to shut off."

Chris made her way to the kitchen, climbed up on a chair and pressed the silencer button on the smoke detector. From her elevated position she took a quick survey of the room. Everything seemed to be in order—with the exception of a charred lump of what she assumed used to be meat, sitting in a blackened pot in the sink.

Ken scowled up at her. "Well?" he demanded, feet set wide, hands on hips.

"Well, what?" Chris giggled.

At the sound of her laughter he shifted from his pugnacious stance. An embarrassed grin stole across his mouth. "I burned supper."

"I noticed." She stepped down and peered into the sink. "What did it used to be?"

"Rump roast. See," he pointed out, "those small black lumps are carrots."

Chris stuck a fork into the meat but couldn't pry the blackened roast from the bottom of the pot. "What happened?"

"I had some business calls to make. And then I took a shower . . ."

"You have to make sure there's always a little liquid in the bottom."

"The book didn't tell me that."

Chris wiped a smudge of soot from his cheek. His eyes locked into hers at the touch of her fingertip. A silent message passed between them with tender ferocity. "Damn," Chris swore under her breath.

"Mindless mush?"

"Something like that."

"If it's any consolation, you don't do much for my powers of concentration, either."

Chris retreated, putting some physical distance between them. "I don't think it's salvageable," she said, turning her attention to the roast.

"I'll take you out to dinner."

She considered the idea for a moment, wondering how to remind him tactfully that he had no job and probably shouldn't be squandering his money. "I have a better idea. Why don't we stay home, and I'll teach you how to make macaroni and cheese?"

His face brightened. "I love macaroni and cheese."

Chris couldn't help smiling with him. "I know." *This is hopeless,* she thought, *how could anybody resist a man who made you feel like a million dollars just because you offered to make macaroni and cheese?* Sighing in resignation, Chris shrugged out of her coat. Ken took it from her and headed toward the front hall closet as she began pulling things from the refrigerator. "Milk, butter, cheddar cheese," she mumbled as she set the food on the countertop. As Ken walked back into the kitchen, she handed him the block of cheese. "You can grate this in the food processor."

His face looked blank. "Food processor?"

Chris moved the machine to the front of the counter. "Cut the cheese into chunks . . . like this. Drop them into the attachment . . . here. Press the proper button—this one—and presto!" The machine whirred.

"I think I can handle that."

Chris melted butter in a small saucepan and added a little flour, stirring with a wire whisk. "You see," she said, "two tablespoons melted butter and two tablespoons of flour."

"Hmmmm," he hummed into her hair as he watched over her shoulder.

"Then, after you've cooked this together for a minute or two, you add a cup of milk."

"Cup of milk," he repeated, the husky words vibrating along the edge of Chris' ear.

Chris closed her eyes and swallowed. "Have you grated that cheese, yet?"

"I was watching you."

"Well, you don't have to watch me anymore. That's all there is to the sauce. Now it just gets cooked until it thickens a little." Chris set a pot of water on the stove to boil.

"Grated cheese and elbow macaroni," Ken said, placing them next to the stove. "I feel like I'm assisting at surgery."

"This is nothing. Wait until I teach you how to make soup, and you have to cut up a billion vegetables."

"I'm good at vegetables. I made a salad," he said proudly. He took a large plastic wrapped bowl from the refrigerator for her inspection.

Chris looked at his handiwork with genuine admiration. He definitely had a flair for salad.

"I noticed a hambone in here," he called over his shoulder as he rummaged in the refrigerator. "Maybe we could slice some ham off it and add it to the macaroni and cheese."

They worked together in companionable silence, setting the table, then adding cheese to the white sauce before combining it with the cooked macaroni and slivers of ham. Chris sprinkled extra cheese over the top and slid the dish into the oven to brown. They stood at the stove in hushed expectancy, waiting for their supper.

Ken grinned down at her. "I guess it's kind of dumb, but I really am enjoying myself. It's nice to work in the kitchen with you."

Chris nodded in agreement. "I like to cook, but I almost never get the chance. I never get home before six, and Lucy can't wait much longer than that to eat." She stole a slice of radish from the salad and carried the bowl into the dining room. "Besides, when Aunt Edna's here, she really isn't too crazy about me invading her kitchen." Chris took the steaming casserole from the oven and set it on the table.

Ken waved his fork at the heaping portion of macaroni he had doled out onto his plate. "I can make this, now: two tablespoons butter, two tablespoons flour, one cup of milk, and a bunch of cheese."

"Is it okay?"

"It's great."

Chris stared across the table at him. "I see you've decided to grow a beard."

Ken rubbed the black four-day-old whiskers with his thumb. "I thought I'd give it a try. What do you think?"

The thought of Ken in full beard gave her the shivers. It would be like black silk—making his sensuous smile even more enigmatic, joining the lush curls that partially hid his ears, highlighting eyes that were already far too expressive. An unbidden warmth spread through her at the tactile possibilities of a bearded Ken.

Ken looked at her expectantly, waiting for an answer. "Well?"

Chris took a deep breath. "It makes you look a little . . . ah . . . primitive."

"Primitive?"

Chris toyed with her noodles. "You know . . . sort of . . ."

He was watching her closely, fork poised in midair, brows raised in question.

Chris rolled her eyes from side to side and

flipped her hands palm up in a gesture of exasperation. "Well, hell. Sexy. If you must know, the damn thing makes you look incredibly sexy."

"Incredibly sexy?" His eyes opened wide. The corners of his mouth curled up in candid delight. "Damn!"

Chris couldn't keep herself from laughing. It had been an awkward admission for her to make, but he responded with such surprised happiness that she was glad she'd told him. She liked seeing him happy. And she was relieved to know that he hadn't grown it because he knew it was sexy.

"The only other times I've grown a beard have been on camping and fishing trips, and my all-male companions would hardly tell me it was sexy." He searched the salad bowl for errant chunks of broccoli. "I've always had to shave the darn thing off at the first sign of civilization." He rested his cast on the table. "Sometimes I wonder what it would be like to make love behind a beard." His voice grew low and seductive, rubbing erotically against her disintegrating composure. He held her gaze with provocative, teasing eyes.

Chris swallowed against a rising tide of desire and turmoil. Her breath was shallow between slightly parted lips.

"Have you ever made love to a man with a

121

beard?" Ken asked, his voice velvety and suggestive.

"Uh . . . no," she gasped. Her fork slid from her fingers and clattered onto her plate, causing her to jump in her seat.

Ken leaned back in his chair. A small frown drew his black brows together. "I've done it again. I've sent you into a state of total panic." He pushed his plate aside and leaned forward, elbows on the table. "After you left this morning, I sat down and made up a plan . . . which I have now screwed up. I thought I'd be on my good behavior for the next two days. Make sure everything stayed platonic so we could get to know each other better." The contrite tone left his voice, and his eyes sparkled with mischief. "And then by the weekend you'd see what a great guy I was and jump into my bed."

Chris opened her eyes wide and wrinkled her nose. "That's disgusting."

"It's not disgusting. It's human nature. I'm a perfectly healthy, sexually average male . . ."

Chris opened her eyes even wider. Healthy, yes. Sexually average, never.

". . . and my life has been crazy ever since I met you. For three days now I've walked around in a constant state of . . . ah . . . arousal. In the beginning, I didn't know why I was so attracted to you.

It was just one of those things that happens . . . like catching a cold. You don't know how you got the damn thing, but it's obvious you're gonna be stuck with it until it runs its course. Now I find out that not only do you drive me crazy, but I like you. I like the way your face glows when you talk about Lucy. I like the way you wrinkle your nose and open your eyes wide, and that you laugh easily. I even like the way you get mad when you're cornered. You're a lot like me. We sputter and stomp and before you know it there's no more anger. I like your bravery and your strength and the fact that you try to make the best of any situation."

He paused and let his face relax into a satisfied smile. "And I love your macaroni and cheese." He covered her hand with his, sending a thrill racing up her arm. "Honey, you have to understand that this is hard for me, too. I've never felt like this about a woman before. I'm not exactly sure how to handle it. Last time I can remember having this little control over myself was in seventh grade."

"Seventh grade?"

"I was precocious," he bragged. "And I thought I was in love with Mary Ann Malinowski."

Chris rose and stacked the plates. "But now you know you weren't in love?"

"I was in seventh-grade lust. And I was incredibly impressed with myself. The only permanent result of it all was a seventh-grade average that matched Mary Ann Malinowski's IQ. I would have been better off if my average had matched her chest measurement."

Chris was beginning to hate Mary Ann Malinowski. "That big, huh?"

"She was known as 'the Wondergirl.'"

"Were there other girls after Mary Ann that you thought you were in love with?"

Ken carried the almost-empty casserole into the kitchen. He lounged against the sink and looked thoughtful. "There were girls that I found very attractive. There were girls that I regarded as very good friends." He shook his head. "No. There's been an unusually large gap between the great love affairs of my life." He measured coffee into the coffee maker. "I used to think it was a matter of time. While I was in school I was always scrambling for grades. I was the first person in my family to get a college diploma. My father was determined to see me graduate, and I wouldn't have disappointed him for anything." Ken grinned. "But it was tough. I'm not exactly the brainy type. I studied until two in the morning, and I still couldn't get the hang of French. I failed courses, and I made them up in summer school. I graduated five hundred sixty-seventh out of a class of six hundred and twelve."

A college degree. That was something Chris hadn't suspected. "A carpenter with a college degree?"

"After college, I got fired from fourteen jobs. I was not your ideal employee. I couldn't stand sitting indoors at a desk. And I felt strangled in a tie. Finally, I said the hell with it all and started working as a carpenter. And here I am. I don't do much carpentry work, anymore, but I'm still in construction." He took the freshly brewed coffee and put it on a tray. "I used to think that all these years I'd been too busy to fall in love. Now I think that the right person just never came along." He playfully tugged at an orange curl. "I'm busier than I've ever been, and I'm hopelessly in love with you."

"You thought you were hopelessly in love with Mary Ann Malinowski."

"True. But you don't have the . . . attributes . . . she had," he chuckled. "This time it must really be love."

Chris sniffed indignantly. "There's nothing wrong with my . . . attributes."

He looked at her longingly. "You have beautiful

attributes, but if I'm going to stick to my plan I'd rather not think about them."

"Maybe your plan isn't so bad." Chris added two ceramic mugs to the coffee tray. She looked into his clear blue eyes and felt a warm rush of pleasure at the affection she saw there. She hated to admit it, but it was nice having Ken around. And it was nice having a man look at her like that. "I'd like to know you better."

He leaned forward and kissed her very softly. He drew away with no attempt to deepen the kiss. His eyes prolonged the moment with a silent, visual caress that lingered on her lips.

Chris thought about the second part of his plan. The part about jumping into his bed, and she wondered how she would ever last until Saturday.

Ken sighed. "I'm not even going to attempt a guess at what that smile means."

"Maybe we should take our coffee downstairs."

Chapter 6

Ken leaned forward in concentration, his right hand hovering over his queen. Finally, solemnly, he moved the antique ivory carving. "Check. Checkmate," he concluded.

Chris pressed her lips together in irritation. For the last two nights he'd beaten her consistently at chess, cribbage, Scrabble, two-handed pinochle, hangman, and Monopoly. Monopoly was the worst. He'd immediately landed on Boardwalk and Park Place, built hotels on all his property, and bankrupted her with such enthusiasm that it sent chills down her spine at the thought of him turned loose on corporate America. At least he wasn't patronizing, she concluded morosely, trying to find something positive in her latest defeat.

Ken moved the chess board from the couch to the coffee table. He glanced at his watch. "It's ten-thirty. You must be tired."

"A little, but it's Friday and I can sleep later tomorrow."

"Do you teach on Saturday?"

"I have a few lessons during the public skating session. And then there are freestyle sessions from four to seven."

"About this freestyle . . ."

"Umm?"

"What is it?"

"That's when the competitive skaters practice."

Ken stretched his long legs in front of him as he sank back into a corner of the couch. "I figured, but I'm not sure why it's called freestyle."

"Freestyle refers to the type of skating. It's a time when jumps, spins, and routines are practiced. When the ice dancers train, they have their own time called a dance session."

"Ice skating is a strange sport."

"I always thought football was a strange sport."

"Point taken."

Chris curled her legs under her and watched Ken. His eyes were turned toward the fire flickering in the fireplace. His lean, hard-muscled body reclined along the contours of the couch, reminding her of a powerful jungle cat enjoying the warmth of the sun. His glossy black hair curled over his ears and joined the close-cropped beard.

His chest rose and fell slowly under a soft red plaid flannel shirt. He had learned to cook eggs, roast chicken, and bake brownies—just for her. He had kept the house neat, thoughtfully turned the porch light on to welcome her home each evening, and kept her mind occupied with games played in front of a roaring fire every night after dinner. He had followed the plan and allowed her some space to get to know him without sexual involvement. But the sexual involvement was always there. The extraordinary attraction they felt for each other constantly simmered below the surface. There were unguarded moments when raw hunger flared across Ken's face and her own skin burned with the desire to mold itself against his hard body—and he would ease the tension with gentle teasing. "Think you can make it to Saturday?" he'd taunt. Chris would assume a haughty look and tip her nose into the air. "I don't know what you mean." And then they would both relax into smiles and chuckles.

Chris bit her lip as she studied Ken. Saturday was an hour and a half away. Her stomach churned at the thought. Nothing had changed in the past two days. If anything, it had gotten worse. She was falling in love. Hopelessly, deeply in love. Every instinct she possessed told her it was a terrible mistake, but she felt powerless to control the direction of her emotions. Just when she needed to be level-headed and logical, she found herself once again blinded by love.

Everything about Ken seemed perfect. Even his mistakes. She cringed as she admitted to herself that she'd actually thought it was adorable when he somehow lost a pot holder in a caldron of spaghetti sauce and didn't discover it until it had been cooked into oblivion. How could she possibly trust herself to assess his character when she could think of nothing but his dark, unfathomable eyes and terrific tush? Shame on me, she laughed.

Ken opened his eyes and focused them on Chris. "Honey, that was such a naughty laugh."

"It sort of slipped out by mistake."

He looked at his watch. "Practicing for Saturday? You only have an hour and a half left."

The churning in her stomach increased. Dessert rose to the middle of her throat and sat waiting for further instructions. She felt beads of cold sweat break out on her upper lip. "I'm going to be sick."

Ken sat up. "Are you serious?"

She nodded, covering her mouth with a shaky hand, hoping to ward off nausea.

"That's impossible. You looked so healthy just a minute ago."

"I have spent the better part of my life throwing

up." Her voice was shaky. "I have thrown up in every ice rink in the country . . . and some in Europe and Canada. I have even thrown up in Japan. Take my word for it . . . I'm going to throw up."

"Dammit! It was the spaghetti sauce. I knew we shouldn't have eaten it." He leaned forward and touched her cheek. "Chris, I'm really sorry. Honestly, I don't know how that pot holder got into it."

"It's not food poisoning—it's nerves. I always throw up when I get nervous. That's why I was so relieved to quit skating; I could never get used to performing."

"Nerves?" His face showed a mixture of concern and amazement.

"You! Saturday," she choked, running toward his bathroom. She slammed the door behind her and locked it. She sat on the cold tile floor and rested her forehead against the porcelain tub.

Ken knocked at the door. "Chris?"

"Go away."

"Open the door!"

"I'd sooner die."

"Open the door."

"I look awful when I throw up. My nose runs and my eyes get all red and watery."

"I don't care how you look, you idiot. Just open the damn door."

Chris crawled over to the bowl and opened the lid. "I can't," she croaked. "I'm going to be sick!"

The wet towel felt good against her flushed face. She'd seen the last of dessert and the last of the spaghetti, and she felt a little better. Ken supported her back with his cast-clad arm. He handed her a fresh washcloth. "Are you okay?" he asked gently.

She nodded. "This is so embarrassing."

"It's a little embarrassing for me, too. This is the first time anyone's ever thrown up over the prospect of going to bed with me."

Chris raised her eyes to his. "I'd like to make some witty retort, but I'm too sick."

He pushed the hair from her sweat-slicked forehead. "Do you always run a fever when you get nervous?"

Chris tried to stand. She held onto the sink and swayed dizzily. "Oh boy."

He scooped her into his arms, cursed the awkwardness of the cast, and sidled through the bathroom door with her. "I think we should get you into bed."

She rested her head against his broad shoulder. "Jump back, Jack. I still have another hour."

His voice rumbled against her as he carried her

up the stairs. "I'll add that to my list of your many attractive features. Attractive feature number thirty-two: can ward off lecherous men while nauseous." He squeezed her a little and kissed the top of her head. "It will come in handy when you're pregnant, again."

"Pregnant again?" She thought her voice sounded small and very far away, and she was glad she was too sick to get jittery over his implication.

He flicked the light switch, bathing her bedroom in warm shades of pink and apricot. "Pregnant, again," he repeated as he lay her down on the bed. "Don't you want to have a larger family? I had the distinct impression you enjoyed motherhood."

She looked at him through hazy, feverish eyes. "Are you going to make me pregnant?"

He sat at the edge of the bed and removed her shoes. "Only if you want me to," he told her softly. "When we're happily married, and you're sure it's the right thing."

"Happily married. The very idea gives me a headache." Chris touched her temple with her fingertips. "I feel awful."

"My official diagnosis is flu." He rummaged through her drawers and returned to the bed with a football jersey–style nightgown emblazoned with the Redskins emblem. "This looks like it would be comfortable to throw up in." He unbuttoned the shirt she was wearing and eased it over her shoulders, groaning when he saw she wasn't wearing a bra. "I'm making a monumental effort to keep my eyes above your neck," he told her as he tugged the nightshirt over her head. "I hope you appreciate my gentlemanly effort."

"I appreciate your gentlemanly effort."

He reached for the snap on her jeans.

"I can do that myself!"

"Darn."

"What about gentlemanly efforts?"

"In the last forty-eight hours I've used up my lifetime allotment of gentlemanly efforts. That was the last one I had left." He gave a distraught glance at the shape of her breasts against the maroon-and-yellow jersey. "The least you could do is be less . . . voluptuous."

Chris looked down at herself. "I can't help it. I'm cold." As if on cue, her teeth began to chatter and goose bumps erupted on her arms.

"You need to get into bed." In one swift movement he had her jeans unsnapped and down to her knees. He pulled one cuff and then the other and expertly rolled her under the covers.

"You're awfully good at removing ladies' pants. You must have had tons of practice."

"I practice every chance I get."

Chris let herself sink back into the pillow. She closed her eyes and allowed Ken to tuck the feather quilt under her chin. It was awful being sick, but it was very nice to be on the receiving end of such loving care. If Edna had been home she would have trundled her off to bed with a stern lecture about "taking care of oneself." And when Edna wasn't looking Lucy would have brought her freshly made crayon drawings and smuggled her treats from the kitchen. A sudden wave of loneliness for the little girl washed over Chris. She felt her eyes fill with tears.

Ken perched on the edge of the bed, studying her with a concerned face. "Tears? What's the matter?"

"I—I miss Lucy!" she sniffled. She wiped her eyes with the back of her hands. "Goodness, just look at me—I'm pathetic . . . lying here, crying for my daughter. I feel like such a boob."

Ken smiled and stroked her hair from her forehead. "You're not a boob. You're just sick, and you miss your family. Why don't we do something to take your mind off it." He reached out and took a paperback book from the night table. "When my little sisters were sick I used to read to them. Would you like me to read to you?"

Chris looked at the book he held in his hand. It was a romance. An engraved leather bookmark innocently rested between the pages of a torrid love scene. Ordinarily, she would never have been able to put the book down at such a spot, but an especially exhausting weekend had caused her to drop off to sleep even as the hero's hand crept up the heroine's thigh.

Aching bones and throbbing head were not sufficient to extinguish the humor of the situation. Chris could barely control the impulse to laugh out loud at the idea of Ken reading her love scenes while she had the plague. It was the ultimate practical joke. *I'm an awful person*, she thought. *His offer to read to me is such a sweet gesture . . . and here I am snickering over the inevitable outcome.* She slid deeper under the covers, hoping to hide the horrible smile that kept creeping across her mouth. "Mmmm," she mumbled, "I'd like you to read to me."

He opened the book to the bookmark and scanned the page. Chris watched him closely, but his face remained impassive. He flipped back a few pages. "Would you mind if I started at the beginning of the chapter? I've never been any good at walking into the middle of a movie . . . or, in this case, starting in the middle of a chapter."

Chris gave silent assent. She closed her eyes in

deference to the pounding headache and lay perfectly still, hoping to diminish the nausea. Ken read in a low, velvety voice that drifted soothingly through the fog of fever. The story was already familiar to her and required little concentration. She heard only a few disconnected sentences before falling into a restless sleep.

Chris opened her eyes to find sunlight splashing across her comforter. There was a moment of panic until she realized it was Saturday and she could oversleep legally. A memory of the preceding night sifted through the sluggish drowse. "Oh no. Oh darn." She groaned softly, attempting to rise to a sitting position. She propped herself up against the headboard and broke out into a cold sweat from the effort.

"Are you okay?"

Chris turned toward the familiar rumble of Ken's bedroom voice to find him slouched casually in the overstuffed club chair in the corner of her room. He half reclined in the chair with one sock-clad foot on the floor and one resting on the ottoman that matched the chair. His red plaid flannel shirt hung unbuttoned and untucked, giving silent testimony that he'd slept in his clothes; and, from the dark smudges under his eyes, Chris guessed that he'd slept very badly. He stood and stretched, unconsciously displaying an intriguing patch of dark hair under his shirt and a tantalizingly masculine bulge behind his zipper. Chris managed a weak smile and decided she must be feeling better. Really sick people didn't get that much pleasure just from ogling a bulge.

Ken sat at the edge of her bed and lay his hand against her cheek. "Glad to see you feeling better. You had me scared for a while there last night. You were really sick until about two-thirty, and then your fever broke."

"I don't remember."

"You kept calling for Bruce. Who the hell is Bruce?"

"Bruce was my dog when I was a little girl. We were inseparable. He was a huge, shaggy sheepdog that loped after me wherever I went. He died from old age when I was nine years old."

Ken looked disgusted. "You mean I spent the better part of the night being jealous of a dog?"

"Were you really jealous?"

"Um-hmmm." He covered her hand with his.

"I think I fell asleep while you were reading to me."

"You didn't even make it to the good part." He smiled roguishly. "That's some book. I always thought romances were for delicate, frail lady types. Do you know there are pages and pages of sex in that book?"

Chris bit back a smile. "Gee, I'm sorry I missed it."

"That's okay. I marked my favorite pages." His eyes sparkled dangerously. "When you're feeling better we can read them together."

"You marked your favorite pages?" She looked at the book lying on the floor beside the club chair. White strips of paper fluttered throughout. "You read the whole book."

He looked embarrassed. His swarthy complexion colored red under the black beard. "You were so sick . . . I was afraid to leave you alone, and it . . . uh . . . it gave me something to do." He stood up suddenly and plunged his hand into his pocket. "Well, hell," he grinned good-naturedly, "the truth is . . . I enjoyed it." His eyes raked across her nightshirt. They crinkled into laugh lines and his teeth flashed white in a dazzling smile of laughter turned inward. "You can't imagine how frustrating it was."

Chris wrinkled her nose and frowned. Didn't the man ever do anything rotten? How could she kick him out of her life when he was such a good sport about everything? How could anyone not love Ken? "Damn."

"Damn?"

She slumped into her pillow. "I practically snickered myself to sleep last night knowing you would be in a state when you got to all those juicy love scenes. And now instead of getting grumpy and testy, you have the nerve to be adorable about it."

"Adorable? Hmmm. I've never thought of myself as being adorable. Puppies and baby dresses and stuffed animals are adorable. Garfield is adorable." He straightened his spine. "I've always thought of myself more as . . . irresistible."

Chris responded with a heavy-lidded smile. *Yes,* she thought, *you're irresistible. But there are times when you're also adorable, and I find it every bit as incongruous as you do. It's amazing that anyone so masculine and so virile could have kept enough little-boy vulnerability to make him adorable.*

Ken straightened the comforter and tucked it in around Chris. "What's the verdict? Is this a case of major flu? Or is this one of those twenty-four-hour things?"

"I think it's just twenty-four-hour. I'm not nauseous, and I don't think I have a fever." She held her head with both hands. "Just residual headache."

"And from the white pallor of your otherwise glowing complexion I would guess you're pretty weak."

Chris sank lower into her pillow. "Nothing two or three days' worth of solid sleep wouldn't cure."

"Do you think you should see a doctor?"

"*No!*"

He nodded his head. "Okay. How about some tea and toast?"

"I'd rather have coffee and a waffle."

His eyebrow quirked over one eye in reprimand, and he sauntered from the room.

Sunday morning Chris swung her legs over the side of the bed and reveled in the glorious feeling of being healthy and rested. The aroma of freshly brewed coffee washed over her in warm, tantalizing waves. Her man was in the kitchen. *Her man.* The phrase almost knocked the wind out of her. She rose from the bed on shaky legs, knowing it wasn't flu that made her tremble—it was the anticipation of seeing Ken. For two days he'd brought her flowers and books and meals. He'd brought a TV into her room, and he'd gotten movies for the DVD player.

He'd stayed with her, sharing her recuperation in a quiet, comfy way, sitting on the bed or in the club chair, and he kept an atmosphere of companionable silence, allowing her to doze and leaving time for her to think private thoughts—mostly of him. Mostly thoughts she had no business thinking. Thoughts about a man in her future. A man who would be a real father to Lucy, teaching her soccer and softball and grilling prospective suitors. A man Chris could talk to in the privacy of her bedroom. Not sexy talk—just regular talk, like "Vicki Jamison drove me nuts today," or "Orange juice was half-price at Super-Duper, so I bought twelve gallons."

It was easy to imagine Ken as such a man. He was the stuff dreams were made of—and she loved him. Lord, how she loved him. It was a bittersweet, lump-in-the-throat sort of love. It was a love she would have to guard closely and keep in her secret heart of hearts because fear of another betrayal knotted her stomach and fluttered wildly in her chest. It was irrational and ungrounded, she told herself, but it was real.

She padded to the top of the stairs and called down to Ken.

Instantly, he appeared at the bottom step with a wooden spoon in his hand and a cookbook stuffed under his arm. This was going to be impossible, Chris thought, grinning. How could any woman resist this guy? She grasped hold of the stair rail to keep from flinging herself into his arms and struggled to assume a cheerful voice.

"Look at me. I'm actually a human being today."

"So I see," he murmured, his eyes full of lazy seduction. "And looking very good."

Ken was peeking up her nightie. She stumbled backward, feeling inexplicably shy. She waited for the rush of excitement to subside in her stomach before speaking. "What are you making?"

"It was supposed to be a surprise. I was going to bring you breakfast in bed."

"No!" Yesterday he'd made rubber Jell-O that couldn't be cut with a steak knife. He had permanently fused two inches of cooked, congealed, totally burned oatmeal to the bottom of her best saucepan. And he had cooked a pot roast for three hours before discovering it was wrapped in cellophane.

His face grew quizzical at her adamant "no."

"I'm feeling better—I'll make breakfast this morning," she insisted. "Give me a minute to shower, and I'll be right down."

He looked relieved. "That sounds nice. To tell you the truth I was a little nervous about trying to make waffles on my own. Sometimes my first attempts at new recipes don't turn out so well."

Chris turned before he could see the look of incredulity on her face. Sometimes his first attempts didn't turn out so well—what an understatement!

She stripped and jumped into the steaming shower. Five minutes later she was tripping down the stairs in a pair of snug jeans and a white T-shirt that sported a glittery picture of a daisy. Her still-damp hair curled in little ringlets around her face. A slash of shadow and clear lip gloss were her only concessions to makeup. By the time she cleared the last step her heart was skipping beats over the knowledge that she'd purposely neglected to wear a bra under the flimsy T-shirt. She was asking for trouble and enjoying every minute of it.

Ken lounged against a kitchen counter and watched her approach. A small tight smile quirked at his mouth, and his eyes darkened under heavy black lashes. "Hmmmm," was his only comment, uttered in a low velvet growl.

Chris experienced a moment of searing panic. She had forgotten how fast he could change from adorable puppy to awesome predator. She spread her arms wide and resumed the role of forced gaiety to hide her confusion. "Well, here I am. Ready to make you a great breakfast. What would you like to eat?"

His eyes burned a path from her mouth to her breasts. "What's on the menu?"

"Waffles?" she asked hopefully, swallowing hard.

"Is that the best you can do?"

"Ah-h-h-h," she quavered. "Oh, shoot." Chris stomped across the kitchen, hands on hips, eyes narrowed. "What is it about you that scares the heck out of me? I walked down those stairs filled with confidence and feeling seductive . . . and all you have to do is look at me and drop your voice an octave and I'm . . . I'm . . ."

"Mush?"

"Mush."

Ken tipped his head back and laughed softly. "I don't think there's another woman alive that would come right out and say something like that." He reached out and pulled her into the circle of his arms. He watched her for a few seconds before drawing her closer. "I don't want you to be afraid of what you feel for me. We have a special attraction for each other. It should be enjoyed and cherished." He lowered his lips to hers and kissed her tenderly. "If we take care of this attraction it will grow even stronger, and it will last a long, long time. It's not just hormones, Chris. It's a union of minds and hearts and secret dreams." His cast rested against her hipbone. His right hand flattened over her back, pushing her against him, crushing her breasts into his hard, muscled chest. "Lean on me, Chris," he coaxed. "Your daisy won't mind."

Chris felt the smile creep through her. It tickled her fingertips and surged through her heart. She did as he asked and leaned into him, her thighs sliding suggestively between his, her stomach flat against the snap of his jeans.

He shifted his weight to fit her even more snugly to him and whispered her name in a voice thickened by emotion. His hand impatiently roamed across her back in sensual exploration. It slid to her waist with increasing pressure.

"I want to love you." His voice was barely audible.

Chris wrapped her arms around him. She kissed the spot on his neck where a few black hairs curled from the open V of his blue buttoned-down shirt. Her panic was gone. It was replaced with a pleasure so intense it bordered on pain. When he held her like this everything was right in the world. They belonged together, and she realized that this moment of affirmation had been as inevitable as April rain. "I want to love you, too," she whispered as she kissed the pulse point just below his jaw, touching it first with her lips and then with the tip of her tongue.

A gasp escaped from deep in Ken's throat at the erotic gesture. In an instant his mouth was on hers. The tentative gentleness of his previous kisses was gone, yielding to the overpowering passion that tore through both of them. Chris gave herself up to the black all-encompassing desire that she had hoped to avoid.

He was right. It was special, and it was to be enjoyed and nurtured. She took his hand and led him upstairs to her bedroom, relishing her new-found bravery.

His shirt had been discarded somewhere be-tween kitchen and bedroom, and the rest of his clothes hit the floor just before he joined her on the bed. She wanted to memorize every contour of his body. She watched his eyes blacken as she ran her palm along his skin.

And then they were joined together and she closed her eyes, reveling in the sweetness of their union.

Afterward, Chris listened in awe to the beating of his heart. He rolled to his side and pulled her close, cradling her in the crook of his shoulder, position-ing her so that he could feel the weight of her body against him. Chris pressed her face into his chest to hide the tears that were gathering in her eyes. She was overwhelmed with emotion, with love that was so strong it squeezed the air from her lungs.

When his breathing had slowed to normal he kissed her forehead. "I'm sorry, Chris."

She tipped her head toward his face. "What are you sorry for?"

"I wanted this to be perfect. I wanted to go slow the first time, but I think I lost control." He pulled back a bit to look at her. "I guess I make love like I cook. The first time I do it I never get it quite right."

"You mean it gets better than that?"

He grinned devilishly and shifted his weight. "Lady, you ain't seen nothing, yet!"

Chapter 7

Chris watched the patterns of moonlight on her bedroom wall and listened to the even breathing of the man next to her. It was odd to suddenly share her bed like this. There had been so few nights of her life spent in the company of a lover. She tried to dredge up memories of nights spent with Steven, but found there were none. Her whole being was filled with the present ... with Ken. No more ghosts, she thought happily. And no more panicky fears of rejection and betrayal. She loved him, and she didn't want to hold anything back from him. All the walls she had so carefully and painfully built would have to be destroyed. Her heart told her she could trust him, and she believed her heart. It was a lovely luxury. Vulnerability is vastly underestimated, she thought dreamily. You don't fully appreciate it until you've denied it to yourself for a long time.

She turned from the moonlight shadows to study

his sleeping silhouette. Even in sleep, there was a strength to his face and a protective tension in his body that made her feel safe and cosseted. It would be nice to be married to this man, she decided. He made her bed comfy. And he was nice to love. Gentle and fierce and honest. She felt overwhelmed at the memory of their lovemaking. She had never shared herself so fully with a man. She pressed her cheek against his bare shoulder and enjoyed the faint aroma of man's cologne and some other scent that was a special mingling of male and female.

Ken awakened at her touch and regarded her drowsily, his hand possessively tracing a line along her side to her hipbone. "Hmmm," he hummed, gravel-voiced, in her ear, "couldn't sleep?"

"No," she whispered. "I'm not used to sharing my bed."

He smiled at that. "I'm not either." He kissed her tenderly on her cheek and the tip of her nose. "I've been so busy for so many years . . ."

Chris nestled closer. She liked when he talked into her hair and his voice grew deep and rumbly.

But he pushed her firmly away, propping himself up on one elbow to see her better. He studied her seriously. "Chris, could we talk a little? Are you awake?"

Chris looked at him curiously. She touched her

hand to his bare chest and felt him shudder slightly beneath her palm.

He stroked her hair back from her face. "It was perfect this morning . . . every time. And this afternoon. And this evening." His voice became husky. "I have such strong feelings for you. That first time we made love it scared the hell out of me."

"Why was it scary?"

"I suppose because it was so intense. I've never lost myself in a woman before. Sex has always been pretty much a physical activity for me. Now I suddenly find myself with all these new emotions. When we're done making love, and I hold you in my arms and listen to the beating of your heart . . . the love I feel for you is so violent. It's a kind of bittersweet pain."

Chris felt as if her heart would burst with happiness. No one had ever said anything like that to her before, and it mirrored her own feelings for him. She smiled at him confidently. "I love you, too," she whispered. Desire began to stir in private places and made her feel vampish with her new-found power. She looked at him seriously. "But I don't want to cause you any pain. Maybe it would be best if we didn't make love for a while." She moved her leg seductively against his inner thigh, stretching next to him. "We really should get back to sleep, now." The hand that had rested on his chest slid tauntingly lower. "Hmmm," she said, "I'm really tired. Aren't you?"

"You *tease!*" he roared. He pulled her closer, and she felt him shaking with silent laughter. "I'm doomed. My life will never be the same." His eyes flashed in the moonlight. "Ah, wench," he whispered in his low bedroom voice, "perhaps I can arouse your sleepy body." His hand traveled, featherlight, tickling her soft, exposed skin. "Like this. Do you like this?" he whispered hoarsely. He kissed her parted lips, while his hand swept in caressing waves across her stomach, dipping lower and lower.

Chris closed her eyes and allowed herself to stretch again, luxuriously, and felt almost as if she might purr. "You're so clever," she told him happily. She turned her head, and the glowing numbers on her digital alarm clock caught her eye. "Oh no! It's time to get up."

Ken groaned in the darkness. "We didn't get much sleep last night."

"I feel like I've been run over by a truck. I'm so tired, I don't think I can move."

Ken sighed and pushed himself out of the warm bed. "Get into the shower and see if that'll revive you. I'll get coffee started."

Chris stumbled to the shower and let the water pummel her somnolent body. She lathered her hair and decided she was feeling better. After ten or twelve cups of coffee she might be able to open her eyes.

Ken rapped on the glass door. "You've been in there for fifteen minutes. Are you awake?"

"No."

He opened the door to the shower and shut the water off. "Time's up, Prunella. You have to go to work." He wrapped her hair in a towel and proceeded to dry her briskly. She blinked fully awake when she realized he was taking an inordinate amount of time rubbing the rough terrycloth across certain strategic areas. "You rat," she exclaimed, grabbing the towel from him, "I'll never get to work that way."

"Sorry. Guess I got carried away."

"You don't look one bit sorry."

He chuckled. "I'm sorry I can't finish what I started." He draped a burgundy robe around her shoulders and handed her a steaming cup of coffee. "Your egg will be ready in five minutes."

Chris stroked over to the wooden barrier and wiped the ice from her skate blade. She wore a thick red wool crewneck under a navy warm-up suit with white piping, a red down vest, ragg wool mittens, and a white-and-gray Icelandic muffler.

Bitsy looked at the cumbersome outfit. "You look like Nanook of the North."

"My metabolism is running a little slow this morning."

Bitsy smiled wickedly. "Tough night?"

"Wonderful night."

"The truck driver?"

"Mmmmmm."

Bitsy's eyes opened wide. "Wow," she whispered.

Chris stared at her friend. "Wow?"

Bitsy nudged her and motioned with her eyes. "Is that him?"

Chris looked toward the lounge. Ken stood just inside the double doors. He looked movie-star handsome and lumberjack rugged. His black hair tumbled in profusion over his ears and blended with the slightly sinister beard. He wore a hip-length shearling jacket and form-fitting jeans. He saw Chris look his way, and he smiled lazily.

Bitsy groaned. "If he looked at me like that I'd faint dead away . . . right here on the ice."

Chris loosened the scarf. "He has the same effect on me. Gee, I suddenly feel warmer." She exchanged wicked smiles with Bitsy and skated over to the gate.

Ken tugged at the scarf. "You look like Nanook of the North."

"That's what Bitsy said."

He looked around the rink. "Which one is Bitsy?"

"The pretty lady in black and red. The one that's gawking at you."

Ken grinned and waved.

"What are you doing here?"

"I wanted to see where you work. A friend of mine stopped by this morning with some more of my clothes, and I hitched a ride over with him."

Chris looked at his feet clad in tan-and-navy ducks. "You're wearing shoes."

"These things are soft inside. They don't bother my toe." Ken turned his attention to the skaters. "Are you coaching? Am I keeping you from something?"

"No. The girl that was scheduled for this time slot called in sick today."

Ken gestured at the rink. "Tell me about this. What's happening?"

"This is a freestyle session. It lasts for forty-five minutes. The skaters practice jumps and spins and programs that they'll use in competition." Chris pointed to a small booth with an elaborate console. "The kids can plug their competition music into the sound system." She selected a CD and punched it into the machine. "Patti," Chris shouted over the guardrail, "you're up." A pretty blonde in a black unitard nodded acknowledgment and moved to center ice. "This is my top student," Chris confided. "She's Junior Ladies, and she's qualified to go to Easterns."

"Easterns?"

Chris made a sweeping movement with her hands. "These are all competitive skaters. They belong to an organization called the United States Figure Skating Association. As their skills improve they move up the ladder in a series of tests. There are eight tests for freestyle. When you pass a test you qualify to compete at a certain level at USFSA-sanctioned competitions. The freestyle levels are Juvenile, Intermediate, Novice, Junior, and Senior."

Chris moved to the gate while she continued talking. "The country is divided up into sections. We belong to the South Atlantic section, which extends from Pennsylvania to Florida. In October, a South Atlantic qualifying competition is held, and the winners of that competition are invited to skate in the Eastern Championships. The winners of Easterns go on to skate in Nationals. The top nationally ranked skaters then go on to skate on our World team in international competitions—

and every four years that World team goes to the Olympics."

Music blared from the loudspeakers and Chris' attention turned to her skater. The girl skipped across the ice in a footwork pattern. She turned and gained momentum in backwards crossovers. "She's going to do a double Lutz," Chris told Ken. Patti whipped past them, tapped her toe pick into the ice, and spun into the jump.

"That's beautiful," Ken gasped. "How does she do that?"

"This is her toughest combination of jumps coming up." Chris watched her skater closely. "Double toe. Double loop." Patti sailed into the air and rotated two-and-a-half times. "Double axel!" Chris beamed. "A perfectly executed double axel." The music suddenly changed tempo and Patti shifted into more balletic maneuvers, gracefully gliding past them and smiling.

"Did you teach her to jump like that? It's like magic."

"Haven't you ever watched skating on television?"

"It's different on television. It's so remote." Ken's attention was riveted to the skater. "Skating always seemed like entertainment to me, but this is actually a sport. This kid is an athlete."

"You're impressed!"

"Darn right I'm impressed. I don't know what I expected to see here, but it wasn't this."

Chris grinned. "Thought you'd find a bunch of little girls in pink tights sipping hot chocolate?"

"Something like that."

"Skating is not for delicate types. It takes a lot of guts and a lot of perseverance."

"You said she was a Junior. Don't you have any Senior skaters?"

"None that compete. Unfortunately, I can barely get a skater to Junior level. This is a privately owned rink and in order to pay the electric bill it's necessary to make money on public skating sessions and hockey. There just aren't enough hours for the figure skaters. Patti trains three hours a day, five days a week. She skates against girls that train six hours a day, seven days a week. If Patti does well this year and gets a national title, she'll most likely leave home and board at a larger rink . . . like Denver or Tacoma, or maybe one of the California rinks."

"That must be upsetting for you."

Chris shrugged. "I'd like to have a Senior-level skater, but it's not a killer. I like the glory of winning as much as the next person, but I also enjoy the satisfaction of seeing improvement." She pointed to a leggy brown-haired girl. The girl wore red tights and a red skating dress topped with a sweatshirt. She moved with a style uniquely her own and very different from the Junior skater. She entered a camel spin, leg extended, toe pointed. She rotated in the spin nine times, swooped down, and changed supporting legs to go into another camel spin. "Alex," Chris told him. "She started skating late. She's thirteen and only working on her third test, but she still has a chance. It's a slim chance, but it's there. If we work hard together, someday she might be my winning Junior-level skater. When I lose a Patti there's always an Alex to get excited about."

A loud whining noise droned behind them. The skaters stopped practicing and left the ice. "The Zamboni," Chris explained. "The forty-five-minute freestyle is over. Now they'll make ice, and a new session will begin."

Ken watched the skaters wipe the ice from their blades and cover them with rubber guards. "Why do they do that?"

Chris steered him toward the lobby where students were changing skates and dressing in warmer clothes. "There's a very fine double edge on the bottom of the blade. It nicks fairly easily and one strategically placed nick can slow you down and ruin a spin or a spiral. Besides, those blades cost three hundred dollars."

Ken raised his eyebrows in astonishment. "Three hundred dollars for a skate blade?"

Chris nodded. "Boots can range anywhere from two hundred to seven hundred. It costs from ten to fifty thousand dollars a year to train a competitive skater. This is not a slum sport."

"You sound upset about that."

"Some of our best athletes are priced out. I constantly see potential being wasted because there simply isn't enough money in a family's budget to provide sufficient ice time."

His brows drew together in displeasure. "How about Alex? Does her family have enough money?"

"Barely. Her father works at a second job to keep up with expenses."

"Is it really all that expensive to operate this place?"

Chris sighed. "I know the electric is very high. I think expenses could be cut if there was some modernization, but the man that owns the rink is getting on in years and isn't interested in making improvements. Frankly, I think the only reason he doesn't turn it into rubble is out of kindness to the skate club."

"Why doesn't he sell it?"

Chris made an exasperated gesture with her arms. "Who would buy this albatross? Skating rinks are going broke all over the country."

"Sometimes people buy things for reasons other than profit."

"You mean like a tax shelter?"

"That's one reason."

Chris wrinkled her nose. "I'll have to talk to my accountant about it."

Skaters began to make their way back to the ice surface. One by one they filed past Ken and smiled a welcome or said hello. When the lobby was empty, he turned to Chris. "They're a nice group of young people."

Chris smiled with pride and agreed. "They're like family to me. Now maybe you can see why I was reluctant to become involved with you. My life is so full. Besides not wanting to repeat a hideous mistake, I wasn't sure I had any more love left to give. I was afraid I would have to take some from one place to put in another."

"I don't think love is like that. I believe in the 'use it or lose it' theory."

Chris giggled.

"Shame on you. You're thinking something dirty." He shook his finger at her in mock reproof. "I wasn't talking about that kind of love."

"I know. I'm sorry. It's my hormones."

He placed his hands on her hips and lowered his lashes in a loving gaze. "So what have you decided? Do you have any love left over for me?"

Enough love to last a lifetime, she thought. *You're as much a part of me as my arms and legs and lungs.* "Well," she said, "maybe a little. I might be able to work you into my schedule on Thursday nights . . . and maybe every other Saturday."

"Hmmmm . . . feeling spunky, aren't you?"

Chris wrinkled her nose. "Spunky?"

"Yeah. That's 'adorable but rotten.'" His attention wandered to the ticket office and the skate concession. "Maybe I'll just hang around and explore the rest of the facility."

Bitsy was waiting for Chris when she stepped back onto the ice. "This looks serious. You look at him as if he were lunch and you hadn't eaten in days."

"I really like him. R-r-r-really like him."

"I know this sounds crazy, but he looks familiar. There's something about those dark blue eyes and long black lashes."

"He's from Pennsylvania."

"No. That's not it."

"Maybe you've seen him at a bar or something. You know . . . bachelor haunts."

"I don't go to bars. I don't do anything. I teach skating, and I sleep."

"You shouldn't tell fibs like that, Bitsy. God'll get you."

"Better God than Aunt Edna."

Chris pulled the feather quilt under her chin and nestled closer to Ken. Sunlight spilled through the bedroom windows and glowed in brilliant patterns on the carpeted floor. "This is nice."

"Mmmmm," Ken hummed into her love-tangled hair. His voice was deep and richly resonant with relaxed satisfaction. Chris had come to recognize it as his after-sex voice. She heard a smile creep into it. "Wouldn't your students be shocked to know this is how you spend your lunch break?"

"Absolutely. Even I find it shocking—and decadent. Isn't that a great word? I always wanted to be decadent."

The phone next to the bed rang, startling them out of their easy banter. Ken rolled away from her and answered it. Chris watched, fascinated, as a peculiar expression settled on his handsome features. "Uh-huh. Uh-huh. Uh-huh," he said. He sat up and ran a hand through his hair. "We'll be right there." He replaced the receiver and looked blank-faced at Chris. "Edna and Lucy are at National Airport."

Chris blinked in confusion. "I spoke to them last night, and they were planning on staying another three days."

Ken stood and pulled her to her feet. "Lucy woke up with a cold, and Edna wasted no time getting them on the first plane out of town. Worried about the new baby," he added as an afterthought while he searched for his socks. "I'll drop you at the rink, and then I'll go get Edna and Lucy."

Chris checked the clock on the night table. "I have an hour before my next lesson. I could go to the airport with you."

Ken pulled his jeans up over his lean hips and zipped the fly. "Unfortunately, we won't all fit in my truck." He smiled wickedly. "Of course we could let Edna ride in the back."

"Kenneth Callahan!"

"Just a thought."

Chapter 8

Edna smacked her lips together in satisfaction as she surveyed the table. "Isn't this nice? Here we are all together at dinner." She looked sternly at Chris. "And it's nice to see that no one's broken any more bones while I've been gone."

Chris opened her mouth to protest and closed it with a snap. Edna was just frustrated. She'd been so busy babysitting in Kansas City that she hadn't had a chance to meddle in any lives all week.

Lucy lined her peas up across the middle of her plate. "I can't eat these peas. My nose is all clogged, and you can't eat peas when your nose is clogged."

Chris smiled at her daughter. "That's true. I noticed that myself the last time I had a cold."

Ken caught the conversation. "I read about that the other day in the 'Health' section of the *Post*. They were talking about how it's a medically proven fact that you can't eat peas when you have a cold."

Edna looked at Lucy's peas. "Hmmm," she admitted grudgingly, "I suppose it is hard to get the little devils down when your nose is stuffy."

"You *could* eat ice cream when you have a cold," Lucy told them seriously. " 'Cause ice cream is slippery, and it goes down easy." She looked at Ken. "Did you read anything about ice cream?"

"I didn't read anything about ice cream, but I know for a fact that there are Popsicles in the freezer made with real fruit juice. One of those Popsicles would probably be just the thing you need."

Aunt Edna shook her head gleefully. "Isn't he something? Right there with the perfect answer."

Chris and Ken exchanged conspiratorial glances. "Yeah"—Chris smiled—"he's something." She looked at her watch. "I hate to eat and run, but I have lessons scheduled for tonight."

Ken pushed away from the table. "Come on, Lucy. Let's get Popsicles, and then I'll read you a story. I found one about monsters."

At nine-fifteen Chris returned home to a dimly lit house. The porch light was on, but there were no lights glowing cozily in the living room windows.

"Ssshh," Ken warned, as she opened the front door. "Everyone's asleep." He motioned to Edna, sitting slumped crazily in the rocking chair, her feet firmly planted on the floor, her skirt dipping between her stout knees. Ken motioned to go upstairs. "Let's go to your room. I want to talk."

Chris crept along after Ken. "I feel like a fugitive," she whispered. She dropped her ski jacket over a chair and sat down on the bed. "Why is Edna sleeping in the rocking chair?"

"She wanted to wait up for you but fell asleep."

Chris sprawled onto her back.

"Mmmmm," Ken moaned. "I wish you wouldn't do that. Why don't you sit up . . . or go stand in a corner?"

"You were the one who suggested we come up here."

"To talk. You don't know what this day has been like."

"Let me guess. Aunt Edna?"

"She's indomitable. She never gives up. And she's crazy!"

Chris held her hands up. "Stop." She patted the bed next to her. "Settle down and tell me what happened."

"All afternoon she told me what a great wife you'd make." His eyes traveled the length of her and came to rest on her mouth. "I already knew that," he said softly. He leaned forward to kiss her and stopped just before touching her parted lips. He stood abruptly and resumed his pacing. "Edna put Lucy to bed at seven and then all of a sudden . . . *wham.* She started with this lecture about how men never bought what they could get for free, and that she wasn't going to tolerate any hanky-panky."

Chris put her hand to her mouth to keep from laughing. The mental picture of her squat little Aunt Edna intimidating big strong Ken bordered on the ludicrous.

He shook his finger at her and tried to choke back a laugh of his own. "You think it's funny?"

"You're just upset because she figured us out . . . and now you're going to have to sleep in your own bed."

"Damn right!"

They looked at each other for a moment and simultaneously burst out laughing. "That woman scares the hell out of me," Ken finally gasped.

Chris wiped the tears from her eyes. "I thought you two were evenly matched, but I was wrong. You're a pussycat compared to Aunt Edna."

They were startled by thumping on the stairs as

Edna stomped and mumbled. "Hmmmph, you're an old ninny," Edna told herself. "Falling asleep in a rocking chair like some pea brain in an old people's home." She rapped on Chris' bedroom door. "I know you're in there, Kenneth Callahan."

Chris opened the door.

"Don't you know nothing about catching a man?" Edna scolded. "After you got 'em hooked, you don't go giving away free samples."

Ken tried to look offended. "How do you know I'm hooked, Aunt Edna?"

Edna waved him away with her hand. "You're hooked, all right. It's written all over your face."

"Edna, one; Callahan, zip," Chris whispered to Ken. "Let's see you top that."

Ken put his arm around Edna. "Okay, Aunt Edna, you've got me. I guess I'm just going to have to marry her." He glanced at Chris. "She's kind of skinny. And she gets crotchety in the morning, but, what the heck? I suppose I can learn to live with that."

"Marry her? Well, don't that beat all!" Edna slapped her thigh and beamed, puffing her cheeks up into dimpled apples.

Chris glared at the two of them. "I might not want to get married."

Edna's eyes widened in disgusted disbelief. "What do you mean you might not want to get married?"

"I've known this man exactly eleven days. I picked him up on a highway, for goodness sake! For all I know he could be an escaped ax murderer from Lorton prison. And then there's his job. When he doesn't have a broken arm and a broken toe, he's flying all over the place. I don't want another husband that's a globetrotter. If I ever get married again, it will be to someone nice and dull. I want a man who lacks ambition."

Edna shook her head. "What a boob."

"And besides, that's the worst proposal I've ever heard."

"Yeah," Edna agreed, "it wasn't such a hot proposal."

Ken looked thoughtful. "Did you mean it about wanting someone dull? Someone that lacked ambition?"

Chris kicked her boots off and removed the heavy rag wool sweater she'd been wearing. "I suppose the dull and unambitious part is negotiable . . . but I definitely need a better proposal."

Ken lowered his voice an octave. "Aunt Edna, if

you would leave us alone for a little while . . . I think I could manage to be more romantic."

"Hmmph. I bet you could. Well, no sirree. There'll be no funny stuff while I'm living under this roof." She turned him around and began pushing him toward the door. "Go on, now. Chris needs her sleep." She herded him to the top of the stairs and shook her finger. "And don't you come sneaking back up. I might be old, but I've got top-notch hearing."

Chris heard Ken chuckling as he descended the stairs. He was getting a kick out of all this, she thought; he must have had some very lonely years to be able to appreciate her protective family so much. Her heart turned at the thought of him spending the night downstairs—alone. She contemplated talking to Edna about sleeping arrangements and decided against it. After all, they weren't married, and she had to consider Lucy. She didn't want Lucy discovering a man in her unwed mother's bed. That wasn't the sort of value system she hoped to instill in her daughter.

Chris undressed and pulled a flannel nightshirt over her head. She climbed into bed and closed her eyes, thinking that life was sweet. And fate was even sweeter. It had all started with some smart-aleck greedy mechanic who had charged her 245 dollars for a glamus. And it had led to Ken Callahan.

Ken sipped his juice and watched Chris as she hurriedly ate her egg and swilled down a cup of coffee. She looked up at him and smiled happily.

"Sometimes just looking at you knocks the air out of me," he admitted, his voice filled with astonishment. "How did this happen to me? After all these years . . . how could I have fallen so ridiculously and painfully in love?"

Edna clattered into the kitchen. "Awful mushy talk for the breakfast table."

"Yeah. I get romantic when I don't have to cook my own eggs in the morning."

Chris wiped her mouth and crumpled her napkin onto the table. "Better watch it," she warned, grinning, "Edna'll cut your KP vacation short."

Ken looked at Edna working in the kitchen, cleaning a frying pan. "This is a short vacation, anyway. Edna says this afternoon we start getting ready for Thanksgiving. We're going to order a fresh turkey."

"Gosh, that's awfully exciting."

"Don't get fresh," Edna called from the kitchen. "It *is* exciting. Isn't every day you get to order the Thanksgiving turkey."

"Aunt Edna, try to control yourself this time—last year we ate leftover turkey for two months. Maybe you could hold it down to . . . ten or twelve pounds?"

Edna looked insulted. "I don't cook *little* birds for Thanksgiving."

Chris shook her head. "I have to go to work." She looked at Ken. "Measure the oven before you go, and make sure she buys a bird that fits in there."

Ken pushed away from the table. "I'll drive you to the rink. Edna and I need the truck to go shopping."

Chris zipped her jacket collar high around her throat as she waited for the heater to warm the truck. "You're being a good sport about Aunt Edna and her theories on courtship and Thanksgiving."

"I'm enjoying every minute of it."

Chris slouched in her seat. "To tell you the truth, I'm kind of jealous. I wish I could order the turkey and bake the pies. And I wish I could spend more time with Lucy. She was gone all week.

She came home with a cold, and I only got to see her for an hour and a half at supper." She wiped her eyes with the back of her mitten. "Boy, this is dumb. I feel like an idiot."

"It's not dumb. I understand how you feel. I think it must be hard to be a working mother."

Chris searched her pockets for a tissue. She blew her nose and reached out to Ken in the darkness. "Thanks."

His voice was husky when he spoke. "Let's change the subject and pump you up for coaching. Who do you have lessons with today?"

Chris redirected her emotions to his suggestion. She listed her itinerary and soon found herself babbling about Alex, and how she intended to change the last thirty seconds of her routine to include a double Lutz.

From the corner of her eye Chris noticed a flash of black hair and swarthy beard approach the rink barrier. She checked her watch to find that the last twenty-minute lesson of the morning was over. Ken had obviously listened to her schedule this morning and remembered when her lunch break would be. She gave her skater a few last minute words of encouragement and glided over toward Ken, who waved and bent to hoist a heavily bundled Lucy into his arms so she could see her mother over the guardrail.

Lucy squealed and clapped her hands in delight. "Mommy!"

Suddenly, they were surrounded by skaters who hovered over the little girl. She was trundled onto the ice to slide among them. She laughed and fell. She was set back on her feet and cooed over, and carefully pulled and pushed around the rink. Chris stood quietly, enjoying the scene. "This is nice. Thank you for bringing Lucy."

"Edna didn't want to send her to school with a cold, but she said it would be all right to bundle her up and bring her in for lunch with you."

Lucy made her way back to her mother. Her eyes were shiny with excitement of the day. "Mommy, wait till you see! We're going on a picnic. Ken arranged it all." She tugged at Chris' sleeve. "Hurry and get your skates off."

Chris led the way to the lounge, where she sat on a bench and unlaced her skates. "A picnic? It must be thirty degrees outside."

"It is," Lucy laughed. "It's real cold. And it's snowing. Great big flakes—but they melt right away."

"You guys wait right here while I put my skates away and get my shoes."

"And your coat," Lucy called. "Don't forget your coat."

Chris followed Lucy and Ken into the parking lot. "This is a mystery," she said to Lucy. "How are we going to have a picnic?"

Lucy ran to the truck. "Ken got a cap on the truck. We spent all morning fixing it up."

Ken opened the back of the truck and a rush of warm air swirled out to greet them. Lucy climbed in and settled herself on the layers of quilts. "See? It has a heater to keep it warm."

Chris and Ken followed the little girl in and closed the gate behind them. Chris sat cross-legged and looked around. The cap was fiberglass, lined with walnut paneling. Snowflakes scudded past the large windows. A small battery-powered lamp bathed the interior in soft light. Lucy's favorite books were scattered in a corner, keeping company with her dolls, Fanny and Snuffy. Chris watched her daughter. This was the most fun she'd ever had with a cold, she thought. She must have spent all morning snuggled in this camper.

Ken opened the lid on a large wicker hamper. He spread a red checkered tablecloth over the quilts. "Aunt Edna packed a feast," he exclaimed.

"Fried chicken, fresh-baked biscuits, coleslaw, and apple crisp for dessert."

When they were done eating, they lay back and took turns reading story books until it was time for Chris to go back to work. She gave Lucy a hug and a kiss and buckled her into the front seat.

"How about me?" Ken asked. "Do I get a hug and a kiss, too?"

Lucy's eyes grew large and round. "Mommy, are you going to kiss Ken?"

"You bet!" She laughed, throwing her arms around him as he stood by the passenger side door. "This was the nicest surprise I've ever had." She gave him a big smackeroo-type kiss that sent Lucy off into gales of giggles. Ken's eyes met hers, and they exchanged looks of tender affection. "Thank you," she whispered.

Ken deposited a friendly kiss on the tip of her nose and pushed her toward the rink. "See you later."

Bitsy was waiting for her. "I know him," she groaned. "It's driving me nuts. I can't figure out how I know him."

"Maybe he just looks like someone you know. Some other incredibly handsome man."

"No. It's his eyes. They're so dark—midnight

blue. And those thick black lashes. I'd kill for those lashes."

"Yeah. He'd be great in mascara ads."

Chris switched off the light on her night table and gave herself a mental hug. Tomorrow was Thanksgiving, and it would be the best Thanksgiving ever. All week she'd come home to a household that was in full preparation for a holiday. On Monday, Edna had proudly informed her that Ken now knew how to make pumpkin pie. Ken had good-naturedly appraised his flour-smudged shirt and suggested that he knew how to scrub pie bowls and clean flour-dusted countertops, but he doubted if he could make a pie. Tuesday evening, he sported a blood-stained, bandaged thumb and declared that if he lived to be a hundred he didn't ever want to slice up another head of cabbage. Today, he'd spent the afternoon with Lucy, coloring page after page of Pilgrims and turkeys in her Thanksgiving coloring book. He had a definite flair with a box of crayons. She smiled. He made purple turkeys and green Pilgrims and showed a decided preference for orange sky.

There had been no more mention of marriage,

but Chris knew Edna and Ken had a plan. They got along in noisy harmony interlaced with friendly teasing and obvious affection. Meanwhile, Ken had maintained his distance, ending each night with a loving but brief kiss at the foot of the stairs.

It was growing tedious. Chris felt her mood changing from one of contented happiness to heated exasperation. She thrashed from side to side, ending in a tangle of sheets and blankets. Dammit, there hadn't been a man in her life for seven years, and now all of a sudden she was in a dither because she had to sleep alone for a week. Darn that Ken Callahan, anyway. See what a bother men are? She got up and straightened the bed, then she threw herself back into it with a "Hrmmph." *And why is he in such perfect control? Why isn't he frothing at the mouth, like me?* She punched her pillow and snarled. If there was one thing she couldn't stand, she thought rebelliously, it was a man with morals.

The floor creaked just outside her door. She lay dead still and listened. Had she awakened Lucy with her rumblings? Chris blinked as the door cracked open and a sliver of light spilled across the dark carpet.

"Chris?" Ken whispered.

Chris propped herself up on her elbows and debated attacking him before he got away.

"What are you doing here?" If it had anything to do with tomorrow's turkey . . . she'd kill him.

He closed the door carefully behind him and crept to the edge of the bed. "I couldn't sleep."

"Hmmmmm," she purred at his bare chest and revealing jeans.

His eyes glittered feverishly as he took in the rumpled sheets and wild orange hair. "You couldn't sleep, either?"

Chris thought the heat had become unbearable. If she didn't get her nightgown off soon she would surely slither from the bed in a pool of lust and sweat. She swallowed and pressed her knees together and tried to sound casual. "I always get excited before a holiday."

"Me, too." He sat on the edge of the bed and unbuttoned the top button of her nightgown. "I'm so excited I'm in pain."

"They say pain builds character."

Two more buttons popped open. "I certainly hope so, because if Edna catches me in here I'm going to be in a lot of pain."

"Maybe you should leave," Chris teased.

"Not on your life." He eased her nightgown over her shoulders. His lips trailed lingering kisses along the curve of her neck as he spoke. "I wanted to give you some time to get to know me. And I didn't want to create an awkward situation between you and Edna and Lucy." His mouth moved just inches from hers. "Honey, I'm so lonely for you. I've taken so many cold showers . . . the inside of my cast is starting to mold." His lips left a trail of fire down her neck as he headed to softer, more intimate places.

"I love you," he whispered.

Chris shut her eyes tight in a rush of overwhelming love. She had felt oddly married to him at the kitchen key exchange, and now something else had been exchanged. Something very sacred and forever binding. She fell asleep, happily wrapped in his arms.

At four-thirty A.M. Chris' bedside alarm rang out with enough fervor to awaken even the most intrepid sleeper.

Ken opened one eye and uttered a brief but effective expletive.

Chris slammed her fist down on the off button.

"Why is your alarm set for four-thirty on Thanksgiving morning?"

"Force of habit. I must have done it automatically."

Slippered feet padded past the bedroom door en route to the bathroom down the hall. "You'd think a body could sleep on Thanksgiving morning," Edna mumbled. "You'd think people would know enough to shut their alarms off when a holiday comes around. You'd think—" Her words were cut short by the closing of the bathroom door.

Ken turned to Chris with a look of utter horror. "I'm a dead man."

"It's okay." Chris snuggled closer. "When she's done in the bathroom she'll go back to her room to get dressed, and you can sneak downstairs."

"I thought this only happened on daytime television."

"Daytime television doesn't have anything comparable to Aunt Edna."

Edna sagged in her seat, her eyes slightly glazed, her mouth hanging slack in her round pleasant face. "I can't eat another bite. I shouldn't have had that last piece of pie."

Ken smiled with gluttonous satisfaction. "It was delicious. All of it."

Chris looked at the turkey carcass with morose skepticism. "We'll never finish it. Not in a million years."

"It was a nice big bird," Edna sighed.

"It's as big as an ostrich," Chris said.

Lucy wriggled in her seat. "Mommy, we've been sitting at this table forever."

Ken stood and stretched. "Do you know how to play checkers?" he asked Lucy.

"Yup."

"I bet if we get really involved in a good game of checkers we could get out of cleaning up this messy table."

Lucy giggled and ran to get the checkerboard.

After an afternoon of games and a light supper, Lucy fell asleep in front of the television set.

"Isn't she something?" Edna clucked. "All done in by Thanksgiving."

"This was the best Thanksgiving ever," Chris proclaimed.

Ken grinned. "It isn't over yet."

Edna checked her watch. "Seven o'clock," she said. There was an edge of expectancy to her voice. Her eyes rounded slightly and seemed to pull the corners of her mouth up into a secretive smile.

Ken slouched casually into a corner of the big overstuffed couch. He showed none of the eager anticipation that was apparent in Edna, but his face reflected the same veiled delight.

As if on cue, a knock sounded at the front door.

Edna stopped rocking for a moment. "There's someone at the door."

Chris looked from Edna to Ken. She sensed a conspiracy.

Edna resumed her rocking. Creak. The chair tipped backward on its wooden rocker. Stomp. Edna's feet slapped the floor. Creak, stomp. Creak, stomp. "Well for goodness' sake," she shouted with a final stomp. "Isn't anyone going to get the door?"

Ken pulled Chris to her feet and pushed her toward the stairs. "Come on . . . we'll answer the door."

Edna followed close behind. "Me, too. I'll help you answer the door."

Smells fishy, Chris thought. *Now what? A giant turkey with a bunch of balloons?*

Chris switched the porch light on and opened the door to a young man dressed in formal livery. He removed his black top hat, smiled respectfully, and bowed. Chris looked beyond him, to the conveyance parked at the curb, and clapped her hands to her mouth. "Horses!"

The two perfectly matched chestnuts turned their heads at the sound of her voice but remained docilely still. Their leather harnesses were attached to a gleaming black carriage equipped with elegant candlelit lamps.

"Don't that beat all," Edna exclaimed.

Ken draped a jacket over Chris' shoulders and guided her toward the carriage. "Pretty romantic, huh?"

Chris tipped her head back and laughed—he sounded so pleased with himself. "Yeah, pretty romantic."

Chris and Ken settled into the back seat of the open carriage and snuggled together under a thick red plaid lap robe, as the driver clucked to his horses and began to drive sedately through the winding streets of adjoining subdivisions. Chris closed her eyes and enjoyed the crisp wintry air redolent of oiled leather and warm horses and Ken's spicy cologne. She tilted her head to see the scattering of early-evening stars blinking behind scudding moon-tinged clouds. "This is so nice. I love this."

Ken tucked the blanket securely around them and slid his hand covertly under her ski jacket, seeking the silken heated skin under her sweater. Their eyes met in an unspoken affirmation of love. She parted her lips in anticipation of his kiss. "I love you," he told her as his tongue tasted her sweetness. "I love everything about you." He kissed her tenderly. "And I love your daughter. I even love Aunt Edna."

She knew he loved her and Edna and Lucy. And she knew what this was all about. This was a better proposal. This was the real thing, and this was going to require a serious answer.

Ken reached into his jacket pocket and extracted a small blue velvet box. He opened the lid and took a ring in his fingers. The band was smooth gold that delicately swirled in carved vines around a brilliant two-carat diamond. He looked at her apprehensively. "I hope I'm doing it right this time."

Chris nodded her head, yes. Words wouldn't slip past the lump in her throat.

"Will you marry me?"

"Yes!" Chris was surprised at the speed and enthusiasm of her answer. She had intended to think about it. Maybe even discuss it with Lucy. She sat up and blinked. How had that yes popped out?

He slid the ring on her finger and kissed her with more relief than passion.

The driver of the carriage tipped his hat.

"Congratulations," he called over his shoulder. He slowed the horses and handed Ken a silver bucket with a bottle of champagne nestled in shaved ice. Ken expertly popped the cork, sending it flying into the night. The driver produced two fine crystal champagne glasses and resumed his clip-clop pace around the suburban streets.

Chris sipped at her champagne. "I love my ring. It's the most beautiful ring I've ever seen—but it's so big. And the carriage . . ." She made a sweeping gesture with her hand. "I love the carriage, too."

Ken refilled her glass. "But?"

"But this is all so expensive. I hate to be an ungrateful nag, but honestly, you didn't have to spend all this money. I love you as a carpenter. I love you even more as an unemployed carpenter."

"Why do you love me even more as an 'unemployed' carpenter?"

"I suppose after Steven and his obsessive need for success, I find an unemployed carpenter to be less threatening. In all honesty, I was only partially joking about wanting a man that lacked ambition."

"I don't lack ambition . . ."

Chris looked into his blue eyes. "I think I worded that badly. I was dumped by a man who placed his career above *everything*. I just don't want that to happen again. This time around, I want a man with a little less ambition and a little more love of life and family—and that's you!"

Ken studiously watched the liquid in his glass fizz in the golden light of the flickering lamps. "There are some things I have to tell you."

Chris giggled. "You'd better tell me fast because I'm not used to drinking champagne . . . and I'm feeling strangely tingly and silly."

Ken looked at her in amazement. "You're sloshed." He laughed, wrapping his arm protectively around her. "I think we'd better talk some other time."

Chapter 9

"Holy cow! You look awful," Bitsy exclaimed.

Chris blinked in the bright light of the skating rink. "I feel awful. I have a hangover. I haven't had a hangover since I was nineteen and nobody told me the fruit punch was spiked at Tina Burger's baby shower." She put her fingertips to her temples. "My eyes feel like fried eggs. And my head is going *wumpa wumpa wumpa*. And my tongue . . . *yuk*."

"What was the occasion?"

Chris displayed her ring and managed a painful smile.

"Oh dear."

"What's that mean? I expected more like wow and whoopee."

"Remember how I said I knew Ken?"

"Yeah."

"And remember we were fooling around, and you said he should be modeling mascara?"

"Yeah?"

"It got me thinking. I could just see those magnetic eyes looking out at me from a magazine."

"What are you talking about?"

"It took me half of Thanksgiving, but I found him. I went through four dozen old magazines, but I finally found the picture." Bitsy skated to the sound booth and returned holding a copy of *Newsweek*. "What really threw me was the beard."

Chris held the magazine with shaking hands and stared openmouthed at the cover. It featured a clean-shaven, neatly coiffed Ken Callahan wearing a crisp white shirt, pin-striped three-piece suit, and hundred-dollar tie. The caption read "Kenneth Knight: Consolidating an Empire." "Consolidating an empire," Chris repeated. "What's that mean?"

"There's a big article about him. He's rich."

"But this is Kenneth Knight."

"Looks to me like Kenneth Callahan."

"There is a resemblance."

"Resemblance? Chris, this is him. Nobody else has eyes like that."

"Bitsy, this is ridiculous. This man is not Ken Callahan."

"Look, this guy has a small scar running along the line of his jaw. Does Ken Callahan?"

Chris felt nausea grip her stomach. "Lots of men have scars on their jaws." She leafed through the article, finding another picture. It was Ken at a construction site, wearing his shearling jacket. Chris reached for the support of the barrier.

"Are you all right?"

"I think I'm going to be sick."

Bitsy threw an arm around her. "Let's get you into the coaches' lounge before you keel over. You're absolutely green."

Chris wobbled in beside Bitsy and gratefully sank into a club chair in the privacy of the small warming room. The magazine lay at her feet. She took the wet towel Bitsy offered and plastered it to her face. There must be some mistake. It couldn't be Ken Callahan. Ken Callahan was a simple sweet man. He cooked potholders and ate macaroni and cheese. She trusted Ken Callahan—he wouldn't lie to her. He wouldn't pretend to be something he wasn't. She took a deep breath and struggled to gain some composure, to control the panic and confusion in her mind. When she was breathing normally, she took another look at the cover. It was Ken Callahan.

A chill spread throughout her body. She shivered and hugged her arms to get warm. "Why? Why did he lie to me? I thought he was some kind of construction worker. I thought he didn't have any money. Didn't have any job. Didn't have a home. I trusted him, Bitsy. I fell in love with him. Why am I always such a fool when it comes to men?"

She took a dripping fresh towel from Bitsy. "Arggggh," she groaned. "My head."

"Would you like an aspirin?"

"No. I'd like a gun. I'd shoot myself in the foot to take my mind off my head . . . my heart."

Bitsy thunked herself in the forehead with her fist. "I shouldn't have told you today. Here you are with the world's worst hangover, and I have to drop this bomb on you."

"No. You did the right thing."

"It's a nice picture of him," Bitsy said, looking at the magazine on the floor.

Chris took the book in her hand. The man on the cover was not Ken Callahan. The man on the cover had a ruthless set to his mouth that sent chills creeping down her spine. His eyes were blue-black and compelling, but they were without humor. "I've never seen him in a suit," Chris said dully.

"That's not what you were thinking."

"I was thinking that I don't know this man on the cover."

"Uh-oh."

"I didn't know Steven, either. I rushed into marriage and found out I didn't know him at all."

"Double uh-oh."

"Why does this happen to me? What is it about me that makes men lie to me?"

"You're not going to make a big deal out of this, are you?"

"Of course I'm going to make a big deal out of this. Peas and carrots, Bitsy, he didn't even tell me his right name."

Bitsy giggled and wrinkled her nose at Chris. "Peas and carrots?"

Chris slapped the towel back over her face. "It's Aunt Edna. She doesn't allow any cussing in the house. She says that since Ken moved in she's been hearing words she doesn't like. Now she makes us say things like 'peas and carrots' and 'holy cabbage.'"

"I kind of like 'holy cabbage.'"

"What am I going to do? I'm so in love with the creep."

"Why don't you just ask him why he lied to you?"

"Because I'm afraid he'll just feed me some slick answer."

Bitsy shook her head. "Boy, I'm really impressed with the amount of trust going on in this relationship."

"It's so weird, Bitsy. Yesterday, I would have trusted him with my life . . . my soul. And now, I just don't know. I don't feel very competent when it comes to judging men. I don't want to make another mistake."

Bitsy sighed and looked at her watch. "I have to get back out on the ice. I have a lesson in three minutes."

Chris nodded. "Me too. I'm working with Patti."

Chris felt him before she saw him. There was a warm rush of pleasure that inexplicably poured from her heart to the tips of her fingers. She turned and found him standing at the guardrail with a wicker picnic basket slung over his arm but the pleasure was immediately replaced by clammy dread. This was Kenneth Knight, construction mogul. What the bell pepper would she say to him? She waved and indicated ten minutes—then willed herself to forget his presence and concentrate on her student. Thank goodness for all those years of skating, she thought. If it had taught her anything, it was how to focus on the task at hand.

When her lesson was finished, she skated toward Ken and decided to follow her earlier tactic: focus on the task at hand. She didn't feel capable of making an intelligent decision about their relationship, so she would simply procrastinate. She would put her priorities in order, and first priority would be to prepare Patti for Easterns. It would buy her some time—and maybe give Ken a chance to straighten things out by himself.

"It's the day after Thanksgiving. What are all these kids doing here?"

"They have the day off from school—this is a good chance to pick up some extra ice time. At two o'clock public session begins, and they'll be done for the day."

"And how about you? Are you done then, too?"

"Afraid not. I'm spending some time on off-ice conditioning with Patti and Alex and two of my Novice men. We have a small dance studio here with a springboard floor and mirrors. We'll work on air jumps and do some choreography."

"Air jumps?"

"Jumps from the floor. Sometimes it's easier to correct rotation on a trampoline or from the floor." Chris pointed to the food basket. "Let me guess. Turkey sandwiches?"

"For the next seven months, at least."

They placed the basket on a bench in the lobby and sat on either side of it. Ken selected a sandwich and looked at it with interest. "There's something purple in here."

"Cranberries. Aunt Edna can cram a whole meal between two slices of bread. One time she gave me egg salad with cooked carrots and mashed potatoes." Chris chose a packet of fresh vegetables and munched on a celery stick. "Do you remember when I explained to you about competitions? How the kids work themselves up the ladder toward Nationals?"

"Mmmm."

Chris kept her voice low to control her confused emotions. She wanted to keep this conversation natural and friendly. "In a week and a half Bitsy and I will be going to Boston for Easterns. I'm going to be really busy between now and then."

Ken looked up. He searched her face for some understanding of her statement. "Keep going."

"That's all. I'm just going to be busy." She winced when her voice cracked on the word busy.

"I understand what you said. It's the way your knuckles are turning white while you hang on to the food basket that has me confused. What's going on?"

Oh crud, Chris thought, *I'm really crummy at this. Good thing I never had any aspirations toward acting.* She looked at him in dismay. "I'm sick," she lied. "My head hurts."

"Hangover. You're not much of a drinker."

Chris felt weak with relief at having succeeded with her fib. She averted her eyes and pawed through the basket. "What else is in here? I don't think I can manage a turkey sandwich."

"I suspected. I told Edna to pack a thermos of tea, and I think there's a package of crackers in there, too."

Chris found the thermos of tea and poured a cup out for herself. She focused her gaze on the steaming liquid. "I really will be busy for a couple weeks. There are several students qualified for Easterns. They'll be busy needing extra attention."

"How long will you have to be in Boston?"

"I'll be there for seven days. Only three of those days are actual competition days for my kids . . . Thursday, Friday, and Saturday. At the beginning of the week they get practice time at the rink." Chris nibbled at a cracker. "All ice surfaces aren't the same, and skaters always need a little time to orient themselves in a new arena."

"Is this open to the public? Are you going to invite me along?"

"Yes, it's open to the public. And . . . I don't know if I'm going to invite you along." She sipped at her tea and wondered why she felt so guilty about all this. He was the one who had lied. He was the impostor. Why did she feel like such a rat?

"My schedule will be even worse than it is now"—
her eyes met his defiantly—"and I make sure I set
a good example when I travel with my students."

"No naked men in your hotel room, huh?"

"Never."

He helped himself to a sip of her tea. "How
about your husband?"

"I don't have a husband."

"We could fix that."

"Mmmmm." She wondered about the legal
problems involved in marrying a mythical man.
If she married Ken Callahan would she also be
married to Kenneth Knight? And if he had lied to
her about his name and his job . . . what else had
he lied to her about? Maybe Kenneth Knight had
a wife. Maybe he had a whole pack of kids. She
looked sidewise at Ken, feeling murderous incli-
nations.

He jumped away from her, instinctively raising
a hand to his face.

The action took Chris by surprise. "Why'd you
do that?"

Ken colored under his black beard. "I don't
know. I had the funniest sensation. I had this pre-
monition of you breaking my nose."

"Mmmmm."

"That's all you can say? Mmmm? Aren't you going to assure me it's ridiculous? Aren't you going to tell me my body is safe in your hands?"

Chris narrowed her eyes. Another emotion was forming besides the hurt and confusion. It was anger. For the second time in her life she'd fallen victim to a scoundrel, and she was furious. "Of course it's ridiculous," she purred, thinking that breaking his nose would be small potatoes. Her retribution would be much more imaginative. More satisfying. More diabolical. She didn't know why he'd perpetrated this charade, but he would pay. She lowered her lashes and let her eyes rake over his body. "It's not your nose that interests me."

He looked at her suspiciously. "You aren't thinking of breaking anything else, are you?"

Chris slammed the lid of the wicker basket closed. "You're cute when you worry. You get this little twitch at the corner of your mouth."

Ken looked sidewise at her. "Are you mad at me for something?"

Mad? She couldn't be any more angry. He'd violated her trust. He'd made a fool out of her. "No," she snarled, "I'm not mad."

"Maybe you just need to relax. There's a nice motel about a mile down the road . . ."

Chris stood quickly and smoothed her sweater over her hips. "No," she said firmly. "No sleazy motels. And besides I have a lesson."

"I'm beginning to think the only way I'll get any time with you is to take up ice skating."

Chris buttoned the buttons on his jacket and handed him the lunch basket. "You couldn't afford me," she jibed. "Ice skating is expensive, and you're an unemployed carpenter." She waited for a reply, wondering if he would continue the lie.

"Just because I'm currently not working doesn't mean I haven't got any money."

Chris raised her eyebrows. "Do you have money?"

"A little."

"Care to elaborate on that?"

"Do you want a full financial disclosure?" His mouth tilted into a teasing grin that threatened to melt her skate blades.

"Maybe."

"I'll have my lawyer prepare something."

Damn! Now he didn't even have the decency to lie to her. He was going to continue this whopper on innuendo and flip remarks. "We can discuss this at dinner."

"Okay." He dropped a friendly kiss on the top of her head—and left.

Bitsy slung her arm around Chris' shoulders.

"Everything all right?"

"Just perfect."

"Uh-oh, I've seen that look in your eye before. That's your 'going for blood' look. You looked like that when you beat Debbie Makovik out of the Junior title. I was at least a third of the way up in the stands and I could see that look in your eye . . . it sent chills down my spine . . ."

Bitsy pulled up to the curb and looked at Chris expectantly. "This is it, folks."

Chris stared at her town house. "Are we here already? I don't suppose you'd want to drive around the block three or four hundred times?"

"I assume you have a problem?"

"Boy, have I got a problem." She held up her finger. "Look at this. What am I going to do with this? You know what this says? Engaged. Engaged. Engaged. You can't miss it. It's enormous." She pulled her mitten over the diamond. "Maybe if I leave my mitten on . . ."

"Yeah, that would help, but it's going to be hard holding a fork. If you're that bummed out why don't you just give the ring back?"

Chris sighed and sank lower in her seat. "I can't," she wailed. "I love this ring. And I'm ridiculously in love with Ken What's-his-name." She punched the dashboard. "And I hate him. The creep."

"This is complicated."

"The real problem is Edna and Lucy. I don't want them getting all excited about this. I'm not sure what I'm going to do, yet."

"Then why don't you tell them that you're engaged, but that you're not planning to get married for a long, long time . . . maybe never."

Chris nodded solemnly. "That sounds good." She got out of the car. "I'll go with that one."

Chris opened the door and nodded a grim hello. She hung her coat in the hall closet, looked down at her mittened hands, sighed, and resolutely pulled the rag wool mittens off.

Edna saw it immediately. She put her hand to her mouth and gasped. "My stars! Well, for goodness' sake."

Chris pasted her best professional smile on her face. "Yes, I'm engaged. Your dreams have come true, Aunt Edna." She saw a fleeting glimpse of emotion cloud Ken's eyes. Hurt? She'd said it with unmistakable bitterness. *Hell, the man isn't stupid,* she thought. *And he isn't insensitive, either.* Chris lowered her eyes to the beautiful ring and whispered, ". . . and my dreams, too." She was immediately horrified at the admission. Why had she said that? But she knew the answer. Partly because it was true, and partly because she didn't want to hurt Ken. She wanted to make him miserable . . . but she didn't want to hurt him.

"It's beautiful," Edna clucked over the ring. "It's just about the nicest ring I've ever seen. And it's big. It's bigger than the diamond Margaret Kulesza got when she married that weasel-faced mortician back home in South River." Edna shook her head. "Such a to-do over that scrawny undertaker. The man couldn't even do a decent job of laying-out. Picked out terrible ties. And had a real heavy hand with the rouge. I don't like that. I like when they lay you out to look natural." She turned to Ken. "What do you think? Don't you just hate to see a phony-looking stiff?"

"Yeah, now that you mention it . . ." He turned to Chris and mouthed "help!"

Edna ushered them into the kitchen. She took the wooden spoon to a pot of bubbling stew. "So, when's the big day?" She ground a touch of fresh pepper into the pot and continued stirring. "We could have the wedding right here. Or would you want a church wedding? And a dress . . . you have to get a dress. I think ivory would look nice—you look good in ivory, Chris. You can't wear white, of course, but ivory would be okay."

"Actually, we haven't set a date," Chris said, shifting her weight from one foot to the other and avoiding Ken's eyes. "It could be a long engagement—really long. Maybe we won't ever get married. Maybe we'll just be engaged for a long time, and then . . ."

Edna looked at her as if she were crazy. "Lord, being engaged makes you silly. Why the devil are you rambling on so? And you don't want to wait too long. A Christmas wedding would be good; the house could be decorated with garlands and bows. I always wanted to have a Christmas wedding, myself. I was a June bride, but if I ever marry again it will be a Christmas wedding."

She was losing control of the conversation . . . correction—she'd never had control of the conversation. Edna wasn't even listening to her . . . no one ever listened to her . . .

Edna stirred more vigorously. The gravy slopped over the edge of the pot and small cubes of potato were ground into mushy oblivion as Edna became increasingly excited. "We don't need a caterer. I could do it all. Little meatballs, and we could slice up a nice big roast beef. We'll order the cake. I know a lady up the street that does wonderful cakes."

Chris looked to Ken for help.

"I think it sounds great. Maybe we could feed them the turkey leftovers."

Oh swell. The man-of-a-thousand-names thinks it sounds great. She could just see them standing at the altar, and he says . . . "Oh, by the way, there's something I have to tell you."

Edna waved the spoon at Chris. "You haven't said much about all of this. Would you rather have turkey? What do you think? Roast beef or turkey?"

"I'm not doing anything until after Nationals in January. I'm not interested in dresses or meatballs or instant marriages."

"Hmmph," Edna grunted, lips compressed.

"Hmmmph, yourself," Chris teased good-naturedly. She peered over Edna's shoulder into the stew pot. "This smells terrific. Let's eat."

Ken cut himself a wedge of fresh-baked bread and ladled a generous portion of stew onto his plate. "I have a few announcements of my own. I'm afraid it's necessary for me to go back to work."

"That's good," Edna exclaimed. "A man with a family needs a paycheck coming in regular."

Chris felt the anger sweep back over her. *He's making a fool out of you, Edna,* she wanted to scream. *According to the magazine article he has enough money to last him a lifetime.*

Ken pushed chunks of meat around on his plate as if they were chess pieces. He was clearly a man with something on his mind. There was a grim set to his mouth that reminded Chris of the magazine photograph. She felt a stab of remorseful panic, knowing that Ken Callahan was living on borrowed time—that someday soon Kenneth Knight would emerge, and she didn't think she would like him. Ken looked up. His eyes held hers for a moment, and she knew he would wait. Ken Callahan had received a reprieve.

Chris breathed an audible sigh of relief and was shocked at her reaction. She actually wanted this man to continue the deception. *This will never do,* she told herself sternly. *You are living in a make-believe world. You are in love with a man who does not exist.*

Ken leaned across the table. "I know I'm in big trouble. The expression on your face just went from breathless expectation to blind panic to total relief. Then there was a brief look of love that made my stomach flip, and it was instantly replaced with the promise of a personality that could be a cross between Jack the Ripper and Mata Hari."

"Funny thing, I thought I detected a few character changes going on behind those deep blue eyes of yours, too."

He studied her with guarded curiosity.

Edna cleared her throat and rapped her fork against her water glass. "What are you two whispering about? Don't you know it's rude to whisper? I can't hear a blasted thing you're saying."

Chris grunted in exasperation and looked at her clock for the hundredth time. One-thirty. Everyone was asleep but her. She thrashed to her side and smashed her face into the pillow. She was so mad she could barely breathe. Ken had spent the night being as nice as pie, reading to Lucy and joking with Edna. How could he be such a phony? Chris fumed. How dare he pretend everything was just wonderful. A man like that should be taught a lesson.

Chris threw the covers off with a vicious sweep of her hand. "He's just leading us on," she hissed. "If he wants to see leading on . . . I'll show him leading on!" She stomped to her bureau and searched through her lingerie drawer. Nothing here but flannel nightgowns and thermal underwear, she dismally concluded. Nothing black and depraved. Nothing diaphanous and enticing. Everything she owned was warm!

She dropped her best white flannel nightshirt over her bare shoulders and placed a dot of Chanel at the base of her throat. She considered her image for a moment, mumbled "Oh, blast," and splashed a smattering of perfume on the inside of each thigh. She combed her hair until it was a shining cloud of golden waves and applied eye-shadow over a heavy smudge of black liner. She carefully brushed on a liberal amount of black mascara. "Better," she smirked at her reflection. She smoothed dark red glossy lipstick across her lips and pouted for effect. Yes, she decided, this should do it. She wrapped her velour robe around herself and with a fiendish grin set her alarm for two-fifteen. Ken Callahan needed a jolt. Something to get him thinking. He didn't deserve to sleep soundly while she was in such agony.

There were no lights shining under Ken's door. Chris listened for a moment but heard no sound. Carefully, she opened the door and allowed her eyes to adjust to the darkness of the room. Ken slept on his back, one bare arm thrown overhead, resting on his pillow, the other arm palm down at his side. There was no innocence to his sleeping form. Thick black lashes formed an arc against skin that seemed permanently tan. His mouth was soft and sensuous within the sinister close-cropped beard. Black hair spilled over his forehead to meet a slash of black brow. The strong column of his throat led to broad shoulders and a well-muscled chest that made Chris shiver with the knowledge of his latent power.

For a moment she quailed under his impact, frightened by the force of his virility. She dredged some of her previous anger to the surface. *Don't be a wimp,* she told herself. *Chin up. Bust out. Courage.* She took a deep breath and closed the door behind her. Quietly she lit the candles in the wooden wall sconces and dropped her robe to the floor. She stood a foot from the bed. The curve of her breasts and thighs glowed golden under the flickering candlelight. "Ken," she called softly. He stirred in his bed. His eyes opened lazily. She stood motionless, watching the drowse of sleep leave him. He held his arms out to her, as if this were expected and natural . . . as if she belonged in the warm comfort of his bed.

"I've come to seduce you," she said huskily, moving toward him. *And then I'm going to leave you hanging!* she added silently. *Revenge is a shabby emotion . . . and I'm going to enjoy every ignoble minute of it.*

"Mmmm," he murmured thickly. "I'm glad. It's lonely in my bed without you. I fell asleep wanting you."

Chris felt the anger being diffused with more

gentle emotions. He always managed to say just the right thing in just the right tone. She sighed. And those trustingly vulnerable dark blue eyes were her undoing. Why had she ever thought she could pull this off? Sheets rustled as he sat up, revealing a lean naked torso that seemed bronzed by firelight. His fingertips touched hers, then moved to caress the length of silken thigh that had been placed so tantalizingly close. Chris heard his breath catch in his throat.

"Chris," he whispered almost painfully. "You're so beautiful."

The world rocked around Chris at the touch of his lips. It didn't matter who he was. He was the wind that rushed past her window on a moonlit night. He was the sun that burned its brand into her skin on a summer day. He could kiss a scraped knee and make it better. He could tell a terrible joke and make it seem funny. And he was passion. One heart. One soul. One need. They raised each other higher than any one being could ever go alone and hung suspended in time for a precious moment savoring the black, mindless ecstasy found only at the brink of sated desire.

Afterward, they clung together like two victims of a shipwreck, dazed at the joy of being alive and together on a peaceful beach. Ken held her close and brushed damp hair from her temple. "Wow," he said, his voice shaky, still hoarse with emotion.

"Wow, yourself," Chris giggled. "I don't know how I'm going to get back to my bedroom. I don't think my legs will support me."

"Stay with me."

"I can't. I don't want to set a bad example for Lucy." She glanced at his clock. In four minutes her alarm would be going off! She leaped out of bed and struggled into her bathrobe. "I have to go. It's been really nice," she called over her shoulder as she rushed from the room, feeling like Cinderella about to turn into a pumpkin. She took the stairs two at a time, marveling at what reserves of strength she could muster in an emergency. She hurtled herself across her room and slapped her palm on the off button just seconds before the digital clock clicked to two-fifteen. She flopped onto her bed with her hand over her pounding heart, waiting for her breathing to normalize.

A tear slid down Chris' cheek at the realization of what had just happened—at the realization of the depth of her love and the hopelessness of the relationship. A debilitating lethargy radiated from her chest. She wanted to sleep until the pain was all gone and Ken Callahan was a distant memory.

But first she would have to put an end to the relationship. To let things continue wasn't fair to anyone. And she didn't like herself, anymore. She had no willpower. No scruples. No pride.

Tomorrow, she thought. *Tomorrow I'll find a way to end it.*

Chapter 10

Ken sipped at his coffee and studied the financial section of the *Post.*

"Do all carpenters read the Dow-Jones so avidly?" Chris asked.

"I have a few stocks." He laid the paper aside and buttered a waffle. "What does your schedule look like today? Do you have any time for some Saturday fun?"

"My first lesson is at two o'clock." She chewed her toast thoughtfully. "I thought maybe we could take a ride out to Loudoun County and visit your monster dog. You could show me this place where you stay sometimes."

There was a flicker of surprise behind the dark blue eyes. He raised his eyebrows at her in silent question, but—although she winced inwardly at the tightening of his mouth—she kept her face emotionless. She wondered if it was Kenneth

Knight who studied her coolly then drained his coffee cup before answering.

"Good idea. It's nine-thirty. If we leave now we'll have plenty of time. Darby Hills is just outside of Middleburg."

"Darby Hills?"

"Yeah. That's the name of this place. People give their houses names out there."

"Did you name it Darby Hills?"

"I told you it's just a place I stay sometimes. It came with the name just like it came with the furniture and all the damn azaleas."

Chris had to smile in spite of herself. "You don't like azaleas?"

"I'm allergic to them."

"Do you own this house?"

He nodded his head, yes, while he carried his dishes to the kitchen.

"Then why don't you just get rid of the azaleas?"

He rolled his eyes. "We're not talking a few azaleas. This place is packed with them. And besides I'd feel like a murderer."

Chris helped him load the dishwasher. "Why on earth did you buy a place you so obviously dislike?"

"I don't know. It just didn't turn out to be what I'd expected."

Boy, she thought, *I can relate to that.*

The ride to Middleburg was awkwardly quiet. Suburban towns of Fairfax and Chantilly gave way to frozen fields and spindle trees, their branches pressed against brilliant blue sky like fine French lace. The highway narrowed as it approached Middleburg, and Chris turned her attention to the venerable houses that lined the road. Chris liked Middleburg. It was a town that had absorbed civilization slowly. It had been spared the plastic tract houses and overdevelopment of its neighbor, Fairfax County, because it was too far from downtown D.C. to be a comfortable commute. The golden arches hadn't found Middleburg. Its shops reflected the surrounding wealth. There were saddleries, and Williamsburg-style taverns, and tweedy clothing stores. A lone supermarket hunkered at the back of its parking lot, looking awkward in its bleak brick and glass facade. The small town ended abruptly. Ken followed the black road for a few miles and then turned northwest, giving Chris a view of the Appalachians. After living most of her life under the shadow of the Rockies, Chris wondered how these gently rolling hills could even be considered mountains. She watched grimly as the fields turned manicured; they were in hunt country now. Every now and then a huge estate could be glimpsed among stables and boxwoods, set far back from the road.

She had decided that she would be fair. Maybe the magazine had exaggerated. Maybe he really was a simple carpenter with his own little construction company. She would give him a chance to explain.

Ken turned the truck into a private drive. After a half mile they approached an electronic gate. Ken took a small box from the glove compartment and pushed a button. The gate swung open. Chris read the name on the gold plaque. "Darby Hills."

"Afraid so."

This was going to be hard to explain. This was going to be opulence. Freshly painted white board fence enclosed pastureland on either side of the drive. "There are cows here," she said, dully. "You have cows in your front lawn?"

"Steers, actually. And there aren't very many of them." He sounded apologetic. "I suppose there are a few hundred. I don't even know why I have the blasted things. I think we eat them once in a while."

Chris folded her hands in her lap and stared straight ahead. She didn't want opulence. Maybe other women wanted Prince Charming, but Chris wanted the frog. You could come home to a frog and count on his being there. Frogs were dependable. The truck slowed at a large, beautifully landscaped stone house. The house was cozy and not terribly intimidating. "Is this your house?" she asked hopefully.

"No."

There was a touch of exasperation to her voice. "Well? Whose house is it?"

A muscle twitched in his jaw. "This is Henry's house. Henry's sort of a caretaker." He thrust his chin out pugnaciously. "My house is just past that copse of evergreens."

Oh boy, she thought. *This must be one pip of a house.* She steeled herself as they passed through the evergreens. Sunlight broke overhead and illuminated the enormous Georgian country house that dwarfed the top of a small hill. "Holy cow," Chris breathed. In her wildest dreams she had never imagined anything like this.

"It just looks big. It's actually a lot smaller inside." He drove along the circular drive and parked at the door, his eyes fixed firmly on the house.

Chris kept her hands clenched in her lap. Ken

Callahan was gone. He'd been lost somewhere en route to Darby Hills and would never be seen again. And she was left with Kenneth Knight—a stranger. She searched for something to say—something that would hide the sudden feeling of awkwardness. "This is . . . big. Bigger than Mount Vernon." She spread her arms in disbelief. "This is bigger than Mount Rainier."

Ken sighed and turned to her. His eyes roamed her face for a clue to her feelings. "I suppose you've guessed I'm not just a carpenter?"

Chris felt guilty at her hidden knowledge. She nodded her head and swallowed against the lump in her throat. When she finally answered her voice sounded strangely thin. "Actually, Bitsy recognized you from the cover of *Newsweek*."

He stared at her wordlessly, absorbing the impact of her admission. A flicker of anger passed across narrowed eyes and was instantly hidden behind a controlled mask. He stroked his beard. "I thought I was disguised."

"Why did you lie to me?" Have a good reason, Chris silently pleaded. Something solvable—like amnesia, or drugs, or problems with the police.

He flicked at the keys dangling from the ignition. "I guess it started out as a lark. It was obvious you thought I was a bum, and at the time it seemed like it would be fun to be a bum." He smiled rue-fully. "I haven't had much fun lately . . . until I met you. For the past six months I've been trying to straighten out my business . . . my life. I had a busi-ness partner who expanded a small construction firm into a multinational corporation and bred graft and corruption everywhere he went. It took me three years before I could nail him on embez-zlement and force him to sell out. For the last six months I've been rooting through every company we control, reorganizing and firing. When you broke down on the highway in front of me I was on my way to ax a man I had always considered to be a good friend. I've had a three-week vacation, and now I'm afraid I have to go back and finish the job I started." He leaned his head against the headrest and closed his eyes. "I didn't like being Kenneth Knight when I met you, so I became Ken Callahan. It was actually only a little white lie. My mother's name was Callahan. Callahan is my middle name."

Chris felt the fine line of civility snap. She made a swift, angry gesture with her hand. "A lark?" she shouted. "You moved into my house on a lark? You seduced me on a lark?"

"I didn't seduce you. Women only get seduced in historical romances. What we had was mutual lust."

He was right, but, dammit, she didn't like hearing it. Lust. It was such a narrow emotion, and what she felt for him was so beautiful and complicated. But she couldn't deny it. In the beginning there had been a lot of lust going on. She shook her head. "Who cares what you call it, anyway. You're starting a battle over semantics to avoid the issue. You took advantage of me and my aunt. These three weeks have just been a diversion for you. Three weeks of lies and a phony engagement just to amuse yourself because you're tired of being Hatchetman."

"The business about me being tired of Hatchetman might be true, but there's nothing phony about our engagement. I love you. There's nothing phony about that, either."

"Unfortunately, I love Ken Callahan. I don't even know Kenneth Knight."

"They're the same person, Chris. They just dress differently."

"Are you kidding? Look at this house! What sort of a person would live in this house? Lord Fairfax couldn't have handled this much grandeur."

"I hate this house."

"You bought it. You must have liked something about it."

There was a moment of strained silence before

a mischievous twinkle appeared in his eyes, and an embarrassed grin spread across his mouth. "I guess I had an image of myself lounging about in bucolic majesty."

Chris was caught short by the sudden change in tone. The tension in her eased a little and she giggled. He really did have a way with words. "Bucolic majesty," she repeated. "I like that."

His smile was stiff. He looked at the red brick monster that dominated the hillock. "A little pretentious, huh?"

"Everything is relative. Louis XIV would have thought this was modest."

"We could gut it and make it an ice rink."

"Yeah. It'd have about the same seating capacity as the Capital Center."

The two of them burst into gales of laughter, relieved that they could still find humor in a crumbling world. Chris finally wiped her eyes and sank down in her seat. "My sides hurt." She gasped for breath.

"You're lucky. It's my heart that's breaking," he whispered. "I love you."

Chris blinked against an annoying mist in her eyes. She didn't feel up to a discussion about love. She had achieved her goal. She had forced him to tell her the truth, and now she wanted to go home.

She wanted to be alone to lick her wounds and restore some order—some peace to her life. She bowed her head and studied her skirt with unseeing eyes. She had expected to feel hurt and anger and resentment, but she only felt sad. She had anticipated this confrontation for days—had lived through it in minute detail every waking hour since she'd seen the magazine, and now she was incapable of real communication. She had rehearsed speeches, but she couldn't remember any of them.

Ken draped his arm over the wheel. He gently touched her cheek with his thumb, wiping away an errant tear. "Why did you ask me to bring you here?"

"To force your hand. To help myself decide what to do about this ring."

He kept the tone of his voice light. "Got cold feet?"

She nodded. Tears choked her throat, and she swallowed them down. "Could you take me home now?"

Chris glared across the room at Ken Callahan Knight. "You're being unreasonable."

Ken lounged against the dining room wall and watched the two women working in the kitchen.

"I don't consider it unreasonable. I've paid my rent through December, and I'm not leaving."

Chris slammed the freezer door and marched over to the stove with a box of frozen corn. She wanted him out of her house. His presence was like a drug, robbing her of her ability to make an intelligent decision. And Lucy was becoming more attached to him with each passing day. "You took the ring back. Why won't you move out?"

"I didn't take the ring back. It's sitting in a coffee cup on top of the toaster because you refuse to wear it. And I'm not leaving because I like it here."

She ripped the box of corn open with a vengeance and thunked it into a pot of boiling water. Already he was behaving like Kenneth Knight. Unreasonable, unbending, unflappable tycoon. *Just look at him standing there so outrageously handsome and infuriatingly relaxed. Damn. How can he be so cool when I'm in such a turmoil? He almost looks . . . amused!* She slammed the lid on the pot filled with corn. "Aunt Edna, tell him to leave."

Edna studied the gravy she was making as if it were incredibly fascinating . . . almost spellbinding. "Well, he did pay his rent."

"Aunt Edna, you're siding with him. How could you?"

"I'm not siding with anyone. I'm just being fair."

"All right. I'll give you your rent money back."

Edna cleared her throat. "That could be tough. I don't think we have it, what with paying bills and buying Christmas presents . . . and I already ordered our Christmas turkey."

Chris and Ken exchanged horrified stares at the mention of a Christmas turkey.

"I don't know why you don't want him around, anyway. I like him." Edna waved the gravy spoon at Ken. "What did you do today to screw things up? Everything looked hunky-dory until you took her out to see that house of yours this morning." She turned on Chris. "What's wrong with his house? Why did you give his ring back?"

Chris didn't know what to say. She didn't exactly know what was wrong with his house or why she'd given the ring back. She just felt uneasy. She didn't want another marriage that lasted six weeks. She wanted a marriage that lasted forever, and the brooding executive on the cover of *Newsweek* didn't seem like the home-and-hearth type. And the fact that she'd started out as a lark to him still rankled in her mind. Despite all his assurances, she wasn't sure that the lark had ended. Chris carried the mashed potatoes to the table. "His house was fine, Aunt Edna. I just need a little time to make sure I'm doing the right thing, and I thought I could make the decision better if he wasn't living here."

Ken lit the green Christmas candles on the table. "You spent three weeks living with Ken Callahan. I think you should give Ken Knight equal time."

Edna stood in the doorway, hands on hips. "Who's Ken Knight? This isn't anything kinky, is it?"

Sunday morning Chris was drawn to the kitchen by the tantalizing aroma of freshly brewed coffee. Edna stood at the counter, rolling out a pie crust. She was in flour up to her elbows and humming happily. Chris looked cautiously around before reaching for the coffee pot.

"If you're looking for Ken," Edna grunted as she rolled, "he's already gone."

A rush of emotion that smacked of disappointment passed through Chris' stomach. "Gone?"

"Don't worry, he'll be back. He said he had some things to take care of in Middleburg." Edna looked at Chris. "You don't really want him to move out, do you?"

"I don't know what I want."

Edna returned to her pie. "What a ninny."

Chris spent the day puttering around the house.

She went to the regional library with Lucy and took her to the playground down the street. At four o'clock, they went out to the shopping center and had their pictures taken with Santa Claus. Ken still hadn't returned home by suppertime so the three women of the house decided to make sandwiches and eat them in front of the fireplace and television downstairs before retiring to bed. It wasn't until eleven-thirty that Chris heard the key click in the front door and knew Ken had returned home.

She looked at her naked ring finger and felt a sweep of sadness for the beautiful diamond, all alone in the coffee cup in the kitchen. Maybe Edna was right. Maybe she was being a ninny. She went to the bedroom window and pulled the curtains aside, looking for the reassurance of the blue truck parked at the curb. "Oh, peas and carrots," she whispered. There was no blue truck. In its place sat a sleek, gleaming black Mercedes sports car. "Kenneth Knight," she said. "That sucker belongs to Kenneth Knight."

After a restless night, Chris took extra care with her makeup, applying a slash of eyeliner and a coating of black mascara. She pulled on a brilliant yellow sweatshirt over a black unitard, then stepped into a pair of calf-high soft black leather boots and looked at herself sternly in the oval mirror over her bureau. "Good heavens," she complained, "I look like a bumblebee."

"Chris," Edna called sharply from the foot of the stairs. "You're ten minutes behind schedule. Get a move on, or you'll be late."

Ten minutes late is fine with me, Chris thought as she ambled down the stairs. *I can grab a cup of coffee and skip the egg and my chances of running into Kenneth Knight will be enormously lessened.* She stopped short at the sight of the man standing in her dining room. Nothing in the past three weeks had prepared her for Ken Callahan Knight in a suit. His lustrous black hair had been cut and perfectly coiffed. Blue-black eyes dominated a clean-shaven face that was set in calm determination. He wore a custom-tailored, European-cut suit that accented his trim waist and narrow hips. The cast had been removed from his arm, compounding the feeling that this was not Ken Callahan at all.

His eyes raked her from head to toe. "That outfit is sexy as hell, but you remind me of a bumblebee."

"Oh sh—" Chris saw Aunt Edna turn from the stove and look at her sidewise.

"Shelled peas!" Chris ground out.

"You're gonna be late," Edna told her. She handed Chris a plateful of egg and a cup of coffee.

"She can eat it in the car." Ken steered Chris to

the front door. He slung her skate bag over his shoulder and held the egg while she shrugged into her jacket. "I have to catch an early flight to New York," he said, shoving her out the door. "I'll drop you off on the way."

Chris slid self-consciously into the plush interior of the Mercedes. *Please*, she prayed to herself, *don't spill any egg.*

The engine purred to life. Chris watched, fascinated, as Ken eased the powerful car into traffic. She had never noticed before how beautiful his hands were. Perfectly manicured nails and long tapered fingers that were adept at driving expensive cars and wielding the reigns of corporate power. "What happened to the cast?"

"I had it removed. It was a little early, but if I'm careful it should be okay." He stopped for a traffic light and motioned to the glove compartment. "Open the glove compartment and take out the envelope."

Chris turned the manila envelope over in her hand. A set of keys fell out.

"I'm going to be gone all week. I'm leaving this car at the airport, and that leaves you with no transportation."

"Bitsy will—"

"Bitsy is very nice and a good friend, but there's

no reason to impose on her. Our deal was that I rent a room from you, and you get to use my truck. I'm trading the truck in for a more practical car. My caretaker said he'd have the car brought out to you this afternoon."

"The truck was fine."

"It was a pain in the . . . bananas. I tried to take Edna shopping once and thought I was going to need a forklift to get her into the front seat. And it doesn't hold a week's worth of groceries. You have to put them in the back, and they roll around."

But it was *our* truck! she wanted to shout. Dammit, that truck belonged to Ken Callahan. She glared at the man sitting next to her as if he were a murderer.

"Good Lord," Ken whistled, "why are you wearing your Lizzie Borden look?"

"You wouldn't understand."

He pulled off Reynolds Road into the rink parking lot and parked the car. He slid his arm around her shoulders and pulled her to him. "Are you sentimental about the truck?"

"Absolutely not."

"Hmmmm." He dabbed gently at her eye. "Then how about telling me what this great big tear is all about."

Chris sniffed. "It's about nothing. My eyes

always water when I don't have time for coffee in the morning."

"And your voice gets husky."

"That's right."

Ken smiled and kissed her. The kiss was soft and warm. It said hello, good-bye, and I love you. He sighed and looked at the slim gold watch on his wrist. "I'm sorry, but if I don't hurry I'll miss my flight."

Chris grabbed her bag from the back and bolted from the car. "Have a nice trip," she called crankily. She pushed through the glass doors and when she was sure she was alone in the vestibule she kicked the trash receptacle, sending it sprawling into the lobby. She stood horrified for a moment before picking the can up and returning it to its proper place.

"The wind," she explained to no one in particular. From across the room Bitsy rolled her eyes. "Yes," she told Bitsy on her way to the coaches' lounge. "He's still living in my house."

Edna picked at the Sunday pot roast. "Hmmph," she said, "it just isn't the same without Ken. I don't even feel like eating."

Lucy mushed her mashed potatoes into a pancake and made a road through it. "Yeah. No one tells me monster stories anymore. Boy, he knew some really scary stories, Mommy."

Chris stabbed another slice of beef and slapped it onto her plate. "Well, his absence doesn't affect my appetite. Honestly! The man was only here for three weeks. It isn't as if he were a relative or an old friend." She forked a piece of meat into her mouth and was unable to swallow. All her fears were coming true. When Lucy's father had walked out, the heartache had been a living, all-consuming pain. Chris had gotten through it and grown stronger because of it, but she didn't want to subject her daughter, or even her aunt, to the misery of having a loved one wrenched away. And this man showed all the earmarks of future grief. He'd been Ken Knight for only two days and already he was off on a week-long business trip.

Chris chewed her meat carefully and made another attempt to swallow. They'd all been so happy without him. Why did this have to happen? All because of her crummy car. She hated cars. And she especially hated the brand-new silver four-door Mercedes sedan that was sitting sedately in front of her house. He must have a whole fleet of them, she thought. A different color for each day of the week.

"I don't know what you're so cranky about,"

Edna declared, shaking her napkin for emphasis. "Here you have a good man who loves you and wants to do nice things for you, and you don't even want to admit you miss him. Ken Callahan What's-his-name is the best thing that ever happened to you."

Chris flipped her hand into the air. "You see? You can't even remember his right name."

"Who cares. It's only a silly name. The man's a hunk. He's loaded with money. And he's real nice. I don't care if his name is Dumbo."

Lucy giggled. "Dumbo. Can you imagine somebody named Dumbo. They'd have to have real big ears."

Edna looked at Lucy. "Talk about somebody having big ears."

"I think it's time to change the subject."

Lucy pushed a pea along the road in her mashed potatoes. "Vroom vroom vroom."

"Is that a car going through a mountain pass?" Chris asked.

"Yup. It's going to Boston to go to Easterns."

Edna beamed. "Isn't that cute?"

Lucy pushed her mouth into a pout. "Wish I could go to Easterns."

"So do I, pumpkin, but I'll be too busy to be any

fun. And I don't think you can afford to miss much more school."

"Will Patti win?"

"She won't win, but she might come in third or fourth. That would be good enough to send her to Nationals."

"When's her long program?" Edna wanted to know. "I gotta admit, I'd like to see her skate, too."

"Her long program is on Saturday. I'll bring back a video for you." Chris gathered the plates and carried them to the kitchen. Edna followed her. "Aunt Edna," Chris told her quietly, "when I get back from Boston, I don't want to find Ken here. If we haven't got the money to return to him, then give him a promissory note. Take out a short-term loan from the bank. I don't care how you do it. I want him out of this house."

Edna shook her head. "I think you're making a mistake."

I don't want an absentee husband, Chris thought. *Besides all my other misgivings, he's been gone for six days and he's never called once.* Chris wrapped the pot roast in aluminum foil and put it in the refrigerator. "I'm going to play checkers with Lucy, and then I suppose I have to pack."

"When is your plane going out tomorrow?"

"Nine in the morning. Patti's mother is driving us to Dulles."

"Ken would drive you to the airport. He's supposed to be home tonight."

"I'm not going to depend on Ken. We don't need him."

"Speak for yourself. I like having a man around. Makes you want to get up in the morning and put on some pretty red lipstick."

"Aunt Edna, we're going to have to get you a boyfriend."

"That's not what I meant at all, and you know it. He brings a fresh point of view into the house. And he makes me feel good. Lord, you should have seen him stuffing that turkey. Never saw anyone carry on so! Laughed so hard, I thought I'd die. I was going to have a fresh ham for Christmas, but I said to myself, no sir. I'm going to make that Ken stuff another turkey."

Another good reason to get rid of him, Chris decided. He's the one responsible for another fifty-pound turkey.

Chris leaned against the kitchen counter dressed in gray ragg wool socks, faded jeans, and an oversized red shirt. She watched a marshmallow bob in her hot chocolate while she contemplated her schedule for the coming week. There were four skaters and two coaches going to Easterns, and practice time was divided between two rinks in the area. They would have to rent a van to ferry the kids back and forth. A calendar lay on the table in front of her with lesson times blocked off. Chris sipped the cocoa and admitted to herself that she wasn't nearly as idealistic as she'd pretended to be with Ken. If Patti did well in Easterns and well in Nationals, her parents would certainly send her off to a larger rink to train. She'd already spent two of her summers away—one in Denver, and last year in Tacoma. It hurt. It was painful to bring a skater this far and see her leave for greener pastures.

Chris finished her drink and set the cup on the counter. She heard a car door slam. Her ears pricked at the sound of a key being inserted in the front door, and an inexplicable anger rose in her throat. She switched the light off, hoping he would take the hint and not disturb her.

Chris heard him sigh as he traveled the length of the dining room. Then he stood in the doorway, one hand at his side, one hand resting against the jamb. "Still hiding in the kitchen?"

"Smelled the cocoa?"

"Heard your heart beating."

He wore a navy suit with a fine gold pinstripe.

The jacket hung unbuttoned. His navy-and-red striped tie had been loosened, as had the first button on his sparkling white shirt. Chris noticed the way his well-cut trousers clung to muscular thighs and fell in a clean line to soft black Italian leather shoes. His eyes were tired. The thick black lashes drooped lazily over midnight irises, and dark circles smudged his swarthy complexion. His teeth flashed white in a five o'clock shadow.

"You look tired."

He dropped his hand from the doorjamb and moved toward her. "I'm so tired, I can barely stand. And I want you more than I've ever wanted anything in my entire life."

Chris felt her heart jump. She wanted him, too. That same chemistry was still there. She'd made no progress at all in developing immunity. When it came to sex appeal, it didn't seem to matter if it was Ken Callahan or Kenneth Knight. She drew her brows together in a frown. She didn't know Kenneth Knight. And what she did know of him she didn't like . . . but she was attracted to him, anyway. She knew it was ridiculous, but, as desire for Knight rushed through her, she felt as if she were cheating on Callahan. Pure animal lust, she reminded herself. Essential to continuation of the species, and a lot of fun, but not one of the nobler human emotions. She pushed herself away with both hands. "No."

"What's wrong?"

"Everything. Nothing has been right since you moved in here. You're a threat to my whole lifestyle and to everyone that I love the most. I want you out of here. I'm leaving for Boston tomorrow morning, and when I get back I want you moved."

"Chris, I love you."

"If you love me, you'll leave." She turned and ran up the stairs, not even breathing until she'd reached her room and locked the door behind her. She put her hands over her racing heart, hoping to ease the pain she already felt at their parting. She listened for footsteps but heard none. He hadn't followed her. She'd wanted him to. She'd wanted him to make everything right. She'd wanted him to convince her that he'd never hurt Lucy or Edna. *Craziness,* she thought. *You're thinking craziness, and you're acting like some immature, insecure kid.* But she couldn't help it. She was scared—really scared.

Chris swilled down the final dregs of cold coffee. She tossed the empty paper cup into the trash and cracked her knuckles. It was raining in Boston. It had been raining for six days. The sky was gray. The streets were gray. The brick and stone buildings were gray. They had slogged from one rink to the other, carrying skates, heavy clothes, and dry socks. Thank goodness, it was the last day, Chris thought. She was totally out of dry socks and falling miserably short on enthusiasm. The only items she had in quantity were nerves and heartache.

Bitsy came up behind her and draped an arm around her shoulders. "If it's raining when we get back to Virginia, I'm going to shoot myself."

"I know what you mean."

"Waiting for Patti?"

Chris checked her watch. "Yeah. She's in the ladies' room."

"Uh-oh."

"Checking her makeup. Patti doesn't get nervous. The deal is that I get nervous for both of us."

Bitsy grinned. "You don't have to be nervous. She's second in the short program. If she skates well today, she'll be on her way to Nationals."

"Mmmm," Chris grunted.

"You look sensational. New dress?"

"Yeah. It was sort of a compromise. Aunt Edna wanted me to buy a wedding gown." Chris smoothed imaginary wrinkles from her softly clingy skirt and impatiently tapped a toe clad in elegant tinted stockings and high-heeled slingbacks. At the sight of Patti emerging from the ladies' room, Chris slid her arms into the down coat that had been resting on her shoulders. "Showtime," she mumbled to Bitsy.

Chris checked Patti's elaborately beaded turquoise dress, making sure the zipper was secure. She bent to assure herself that Patti's skate laces were properly tucked into her white boots.

Patti smiled calmly and walked to rinkside beside Chris. Chris looked at the pretty blonde and thought how different each skater's personality was. As a competitor, Chris had been a bundle of raw nerves—she couldn't remember enjoying a single competition. Patti was just the opposite; Patti was a brick. In fact, that was part of her problem as a skater—she lacked that special spark that made people sit up in their seats when she was performing. And then there was Alex . . . Alex loved it all. Alex was a first-class ham. She said that her favorite thing in life was waiting at the gate to hear her name announced over the loudspeaker, then skating out to center ice with everyone watching only her. It showed, too. She always left the gate with a radiant smile that immediately won people's hearts.

The announcer called out the names of the four Junior women who were still waiting to skate. "Juli Schaller, Suzanne Weiss, Patti Barr, and Audrey MacIntyre, please take the ice for your warm-up."

Chris took the rubber skate guards from Patti and moved to a position at the barrier where she could act as coach. Patti stroked around the rink twice forward, twice backward, and glided to a stop in front of Chris.

"A few fast single jumps and spins and go right to the triple Salchow," Chris told her.

Patti watched the three other women for a moment. Juli was the one to beat. She'd come in first in short. She always came in first.

Chris frowned. She didn't like her skaters to dwell on the virtues and weaknesses of their competition. "Skate your best," she told Patti. "Skate for yourself."

Patti knew her coach's philosophy. "Just checking out their dresses . . ." She winked as she skated away to mid-ice.

Chris relaxed a little. Patti would do fine. She was a consistent skater. "Double axel, double toe," Chris called out. "Perfect," she smiled as the young girl glided past. "Nice warm-up." She threw a coat over Patti's shoulders and escorted her back to the lobby.

Patti would skate third. Junior women skated to a three-and-a-half-minute program which meant that Patti would go on in about fifteen minutes. The two women sat side by side in companionable silence. There were some skaters who needed to be amused while they waited, but Patti wasn't one of them. Chris turned to her own thoughts, mentally organizing a Christmas list to keep her mind busy. A cardigan sweater for Aunt Edna. A little tin of homemade cookies and a packet of stickers for each of her students. Lucy was getting a bicycle and clothes for her doll. Reluctantly she thought of Ken. What did you give to a millionaire for Christmas? If there was something he wanted . . . he'd have already bought it. The only things left to buy him would be things he didn't want.

Bitsy motioned from the doorway that it was time for Patti.

"Here we go." Chris smiled. "Knock 'em dead."

Patti gave her a thumbs-up sign, skated to center ice and assumed her opening position. As the first dramatic strains of the music filled the arena, Patti stroked out. Three-and-a-half minutes later, Chris choked back tears of happiness and relief over a perfectly executed program. There was no doubt about it—Patti had gotten her ticket to Nationals. Chris watched her skater gliding across the ice accepting sprays of flowers. A little red-haired girl was lifted up onto the barrier. She held out a bouquet and received an enthusiastic hug from Patti. It was Lucy! Chris grabbed Bitsy's arm. "That's Lucy!"

Bitsy squinted across the rink. "Looks like the whole family's here."

Chris felt the color drain from her face as she stood rooted to the spot in stunned panic, fighting to control her swirling emotions, seeing no one but Kenneth Knight.

Bitsy poked Chris in the ribs. "Wave," she ordered.

Chris pasted her best professional smile onto her numb face and moved her hand weakly in the air. "I can't get rid of him," she said. "As hard as I try, I just can't get rid of him. He keeps hanging around doing nice things."

"How awful. It must be terrible to have a handsome, sexy millionaire always doing nice things for you."

"Yeah . . . and I'm going to put a stop to it."

Bitsy rolled her eyes and thunked her forehead with her fist. "Unh!" she grunted.

Chris and Patti stood together while they waited to read the judges' cards. As the numbers came up, Chris did some fast calculations. Her mouth dropped open. "I can't believe it! Second." She hugged Patti. "You're going to come in second overall."

Chris felt a tug at her skirt. "Mommy!" The little girl hurled herself into Chris' arms. "I missed you. Patti skated be-ooo-tiful. Are you surprised to see us here?"

"Yes. It's a wonderful surprise. I missed you, too."

"Ken brought us. We flew up this morning."

"Mmmm. That was nice of Ken." Reluctantly, Chris turned her attention to Ken. He wore a black pea coat with a bright red scarf and dressy black wool slacks. He stared down at her, his expression unreadable.

"Ken said he'd take us to a late supper," Edna rattled. "Don't that sound fancy? Lucy napped all afternoon so she could stay up."

Chris squeezed Lucy's and Edna's hands. "It sounds great. I've been so lonely without you guys." She hugged Edna and Lucy. "Gosh, it's good to see you." She purposely kept her eyes on her daughter, avoiding another visual confrontation with Ken. She wanted to kiss him and hug him, too. She wanted to tell him how she'd missed him, how she'd wanted his support before Patti skated. But she wouldn't say any of those things. She would do what she knew in her heart was right— she would be cool and discouraging. She adjusted the collar on Lucy's coat. *I missed a man who doesn't exist*, she told herself. *Ken Callahan Knight is a whole person. You can't separate the Callahan from the Knight. Ken Callahan Knight is a person I hardly know.* She felt a firm hand under her arm, pulling her into a more upright position.

"Very nice job of avoiding me," Ken observed, "but I think we might be in the way here. You'd probably like to talk to your skater's parents for a few minutes. We'll meet you in the lobby."

Chris winced under the businesslike tone and biting words. She gave her daughter one last kiss and reluctantly left her to find Mr. and Mrs. Barr.

Ken took Edna's key and opened her door. "Here you are, Aunt Edna. Chris and Lucy are down the hall in three forty-five in case you need anything."

"I'll be fine. Some people complain they can't sleep in a strange bed. Not me. I just conk off anywhere. I could sleep on a rock."

Chris and Lucy kissed Edna good night, and Ken solemnly escorted them to their room.

Ken opened the door and patted Lucy on the head. "How about getting ready for bed, moppet. I'd like to talk to your mother."

Chris felt herself slump. She was tired. She was wet. She was elated. She was depressed. She was no match for Ken Callahan Knight. She looked at him blankly and wondered what on earth he wanted to talk about. At the restaurant, he'd been pleasant but distant. There had been no talk of marriage or love. There had been no loving glances or intimate asides. She wasn't sure if it had been a relief or a disappointment. She wasn't sure about anything.

Ken took her purse from her shoulder and fished through it. He extracted her key ring and looked at it a moment. Chris knew he was recalling the kitchen key exchange, and she wondered if he'd been as moved by it as she had. Probably not, she thought. It had been a lark . . . remember? And how did he feel now—had it become something precious? She couldn't tell by the guarded expression on his face. He returned her bag to her shoulder and worked a key onto the ring.

"I've moved out." His voice was flat. No raspy sexiness. No gentle teasing or enfolding affection. It was a matter-of-fact statement that knocked the air out of Chris' lungs and left only burning, searing pain. He took her hand and closed her fingers around the key ring. Warm, Chris thought sadly. His hands were always so nice and warm . . . and she felt so cold. He looked as if he might say something else, but then he turned abruptly and walked to the elevator—never looking back. The elevator doors closed behind him, and Chris watched the floors blink in red as he descended to the lobby.

Chapter 11

At five-ten Monday morning Chris pulled the silver Mercedes into the dark parking lot of the ice rink. She took the key from the ignition and slouched deep into the seat. *I hate to admit it,* she sighed, *but I'm going to miss this car.* It's definitely a superior machine—it's pretty, and it's comfy, and everything works. In four days she could cash in her savings bond and buy a car of her own. Then she would have to return the Mercedes to Ken. How would she ever do that? she groaned. If she had to face him she was sure she'd do something stupid and maudlin . . . like burst into tears. Maybe she could get Bitsy to follow her out to Darby Hills and just leave the darn thing at his front gate.

A large pickup truck rolled into the space next to her. Its inhabitants cut the engine and waved. They looked around the lot and settled back with containers of coffee. That was strange. Only skaters were usually here at this hour of the morning. She scanned the parking area and realized that there were no familiar cars. An odd sinking feeling settled in the pit of her stomach—the sort of feeling she might get showing up for a party on time but a day late, or if she'd accidentally gone to the supermarket in her bedroom slippers. Maybe they were having problems with the ice, Chris reasoned. Every now and then the ancient compressor or decrepit Zamboni would break, and the rink manager would have to cancel skating until repairs could be made.

Chris stopped at the front door and read the professionally made sign. The rink was closed for alterations and would reopen under new management in a week. Chris was dumbfounded. There had been no warnings, no rumors. She had a skater en route to Nationals, and she didn't have a skating rink. She rested her forehead against the glass door. When things started to go sour, they certainly went all the way . . .

She heard the familiar growl of a Nissan pickup and wheeled around to see Ken park the truck and spring from the cab, a massive set of keys jangling in his hand. With a grim set to his jaw, he opened the front door and pulled Chris inside.

Without saying a word, he walked directly to the office and switched on the parking lot lights. He flipped on the rink lights and the lobby heater.

Chris still stood in the office doorway. "Let me guess. You bought the rink."

"Yes."

"Why?"

"I needed a tax break, and I thought this would be more fun than Darby Hills."

Chris felt a bewildering flood of emotions rushing through her: joy at seeing him; anger that her agony would be prolonged indefinitely; fear over her inability to resist him; and, perhaps most immediate, anxiety bordering on terror that her skaters wouldn't have a home. Chris swallowed and ordered her heart to stop racing. "What do you plan to do with the rink?"

"Operate it at a loss . . . at least in the beginning." He moved with efficient determination, his mouth unsmiling, his eyes glacier blue and just as cold. He pulled a contract out of his briefcase. "I'm offering you a job as head coach. I'm prepared to offer you a salary for helping me with scheduling and organizational problems. The rink will own exclusive rights to your services. The rink will take fifteen percent of all earnings from private and group lessons and in exchange will do book-keeping, provide medical insurance, retirement benefits, and so on. You can read over the terms. The other coaches will get similar contracts, with the exception of salary."

Chris stared, dazed, at the cool businessman standing in front of her. He looked like Ken Callahan in jeans and a navy hooded sweatshirt, but, without a shadow of a doubt, this man was Knight.

He took a schedule card from the top of the desk. "The other coaches will have the week off with pay. If you accept the job, you can begin now by drawing up a tentative schedule. The hockey teams have been notified and relocated to other rinks. It's up to you whether we have public skating or not. I know you get a lot of your young skaters through learn-to-skate group lessons. You might want to keep a few public skating sessions so those kids and their parents can hack around together."

Chris made an effort to subdue the excitement that was gurgling in her chest. If she understood correctly, he was turning the rink into a training facility for competitive skaters. She could finally get her skaters enough ice time to keep them here! The joy was lessened by the suspicion that this was all for her, that he was just being nice, again. She stuffed her hands into her jacket pockets. "You're doing this for me, aren't you?"

His reaction was angry and abrupt. "I'm doing this for myself. It's a tax break. It's a toy. Sign the contract if you want the job. I'll be here for the rest of the day to get things started. Tomorrow, I leave for Chicago and my foreman will complete the renovation. If you have any questions, I'll be out by the ice. We're installing a new ceiling that eventually should cut down on the electric bill."

Chris turned away, blinking back tears. She was relieved to hear the office door close and his long strides disappear in the direction of the rink. She clenched her fists and shut her eyes tight. Well, he was following her directions. He had moved out of her house, and he had disengaged himself emotionally from her life. It was what she'd wanted then—and still wanted now—but she couldn't help feeling a terrible sense of loss. She looked at the closed door and knew that this was her doing. She'd sent him away. But the speed and the extent of his disentanglement was shocking. What really hurt the most was the undeniable fact that she'd been right. Knight had squashed Callahan like a bug—just as she'd known he eventually would. Knight was cold and selfish and ruthlessly strong. Chris looked at the contract she held in her fist. She narrowed her eyes at the jumble of printed words. "Okay," she breathed, "I can do this. I can deal with

Kenneth Knight." Unclenching her fists, she smoothed the wrinkles from the pieces of paper and threw the office door open, almost knocking a painter off his ladder. "Excuse me."

The man clung to the doorjamb. "You must be the redhead that breaks people's bones. I've been warned about you."

Chris gnashed her teeth and growled, "Where is he?"

The painter smiled and pointed to the rink. "I think he's hanging ceiling."

Chris marched to the ice surface. Several men were on scaffolding, struggling to place slabs of aluminum-covered styrofoam on a gridwork of metal girders. Chris stomped to the scaffold holding Ken and gave it a kick.

He grabbed a metal handrail and looked down at her in annoyed surprise.

"I'm not paying fifteen percent to the rink," she told him. "I'll only pay ten."

"You're paying ten now, and you're not getting any benefits. It's costing you a fortune to buy your own medical and life insurance. If you sit down and figure it out, you'll see that you're better off under my management."

"Ten percent."

"Fifteen."

"Take it and stick it—"

He glared down at her. His voice was lethally calm. "You have some very talented, very nice young people depending on you to be here when this rink opens. And you have an obligation to help Patti through Nationals. It may not have occurred to you, yet, but I've got you by the short hairs. This is the only show in town. You train your skaters at this rink or not at all. These kids aren't going to travel to Baltimore to train every day, and they can't be accommodated at the other Virginia rinks."

"You're disgusting."

"So I've been told ... and don't forget ruthless. Even *Newsweek* said I was ruthless." A muscle worked in his jaw. "Is there anything else?"

"Have you been telling people I break bones?" she hissed.

"Most of these men are my friends. I felt they needed to be warned."

"What else did you tell them about me?"

"To treat you with respect and to stay far away ... and never *ever* to stop and help you on the highway."

Chris glowered at him for a second, then turned on her heel and swished from the rink. "Hideous, insufferable son of a beet," she ground out. She slammed the contract down on the office desk and slashed her name across the bottom. Kenneth Knight, she fumed. The man was lower than slime! He was using her sense of responsibility to make her sign a superior contract. What nerve. She paced the office like a caged lioness. She threw the office door open and stormed back to the rink. She approached Ken's scaffold and gave it another kick.

Ken scrambled to maintain his balance, reaching frantically for the handrail. "What the devil? Now what?" He scowled down at Chris.

"I . . . you . . . unk!" She threw her hands into the air in exasperation.

"Could you be more precise?"

"Fiend!"

"Two weeks ago you told me I was adorable."

"Ken Callahan was adorable. Kenneth Knight is unscrupulous and despicable."

His black brows drew together. His eyes changed from ice blue to ebony as he swung lithely down from the platform at the top of the scaffolding to the ice. "Ken Callahan and Kenneth Knight are the same person. You're inventing a double identity and creating a mythical bad guy because you're scared to commit yourself to a permanent relationship. I might be despicable in your eyes, but I'm not unscrupulous. I presented you with a good contract."

"I know that, and I think it was rotten of you."

He ran his hand through his hair. "I think I'm beginning to understand this conversation, and it scares the hell out of me. Do you suppose convoluted reasoning can be catching? Like the plague?"

Chris narrowed her eyes and made a fist. "Do you suppose you could catch a knuckle sandwich!"

Ken bowed his head and held his hand up. "Stop." He looked at Chris from under menacing lowered lashes. "I'm not going to stand here and fight with you. I have too many things to do today." He took a grip on her upper arm and guided her to the lobby door. "I want you to go into the office and have a cup of coffee, and when you've calmed down enough to hold a pencil without snapping it in half, you can make up a schedule."

"I don't need a cup of coffee to make me calm," she shouted. "I'm perfectly calm right now."

"Yes, I can see that by the smoke coming out of your ears," he said dryly. He loosened his grip on her arms and watched her for a moment. There was a sadness, a tiredness to his eyes that Chris hadn't noticed before. It seemed incongruous with the small half smile that curved his mouth. "Actually, I'd like a cup, and I'd be eternally grateful if you'd start a pot going. One of those cartons just outside the box office should contain a new coffee maker."

"Hmmph."

The smile widened just a bit. "I know I've got you when you resort to hmmph. That's as good as a grudging yes."

Chris sighed and made her way through a maze of tools and cardboard boxes. He knew her too well. He knew what grunts and sighs and other unintelligible signals meant. He was no dope, and she'd never made much of an effort to hide her emotions from him. Hmmph was definitely a grudging yes. If he'd been a different sort of person . . . if he'd really been Callahan . . . that intuition would have been an asset. In Knight's talons it was just one more thing to worry about. Chris looked at the labels on the boxes. Computer equipment. A new sound system. He was installing a new ceiling. It took time to order this sort of stuff, Chris thought. He must have bought the rink weeks ago, when he first saw the place. Devious, Chris snorted. The man was filled with secrets and covert activities. She sorted through the boxes until she found one marked COFFEE MAKER. A supermarket bag containing coffee and filters and paper cups had been set atop the coffee-maker box. Sneaky but organized, she concluded— qualities essential for corporate success.

A half hour later, Chris sat with her fingers curled around a mug of cold coffee, concentrating on the scheduling sheet in front of her. She'd been interrupted twice—once to decide upon colors for the lobby and once to give her approval on a new trampoline. It was like Christmas. No, it was better than Christmas—it was a coach's dream come true. It didn't matter who owned the rink, she told herself, or what his motives were for buying it. So what if it was just another lark? Who cared if it was just a tax shelter? Northern Virginia was finally going to have a first-rate training center. She slumped in her seat. So why did she feel so crummy? Love is the pits, she decided. It ruins everything.

The office door opened and Ken entered with a rush of cold air. He looked at Chris for a moment, assessing her mood. He rubbed his hands together to warm them and moved toward the coffee pot. "How can anyone skate in there? It's freezing."

"We need a new heater."

"I think this would have been cheaper if I'd just started from the ground up and built a brand-new arena." He poured himself a cup of coffee and sipped at it appreciatively. "Good coffee."

Chris folded her hands on the desk and made an effort to control the jumble of emotions squeezing at her heart. "I've almost completed the schedule. I've kept the afternoon public session on Friday, Saturday, and Sunday. That leaves an equivalent block of time Monday, Tuesday, Wednesday, and Thursday for group lessons."

Ken stared into his coffee. "Fine."

"Gosh. So much enthusiasm. So much emotion," Chris chided.

He looked at her over the top of his coffee cup. A flame flickered in blue-black eyes. "Would you like to see some emotion?"

Chris felt her stomach flip. "Uh . . ." She blinked under his riveting gaze, unable to formulate a retort. The tension stretched between them, joining them together in breathless suspense. Chris licked dry lips. She saw Ken's attention waver. A small look of annoyance skimmed across his brow and was immediately replaced with one of incredulity as he stared past her and focused on the open office door.

Chris turned to see what had saved her from certain suffocation. "Aunt Edna?"

"Oh my God," Ken said. "She's got my mom with her."

The two women stood side by side in the small office. They seemed about the same age and were of comparable build. Good sturdy sausages wearing sensible shoes and warm woolen coats. Edna glared at her niece defensively, her expression silently communicating. "This isn't my fault and don't you dare say otherwise!" Mrs. Knight smiled warmly.

Edna pressed her lips together. "Margaret, this is my niece, Chris Nelson. Chris, I'd like you to meet Mrs. Knight." Edna rolled her eyes. "This here's Ken's mother . . . all the way from Pennsylvania."

Mrs. Knight extended her hand. "I hope I didn't come at an awkward time."

Chris smiled warmly at the woman and shook her hand. She cocked an eyebrow at Edna.

Edna bobbed her head up and down and tapped her foot on the rubberized carpet. "It was just after Thanksgiving. You remember when your mom called, Ken? She called to say happy Thanksgiving and you never seemed to be home when she called, and we got to talking and having a wonderful conversation. And so, of course, I told her about you being engaged, and all. And how it would be nice if she came down to meet Chris, here . . . and we could all plan the wedding together." Edna's eyes narrowed pugnaciously. "And then in all the excitement, danged if I didn't forget!"

Ken shifted behind Chris. "Sounds like a setup," he whispered into her hair.

"Mmmmmm," she murmured, more in response to his proximity than to his statement.

Mrs. Knight smiled at her son and held out her arms. "It's so good to see you. You don't come home enough."

Ken hugged his mother and returned the smile. Some of the strain left his eyes as laugh lines crinkled in the corners. "You don't fool me for a minute. You're in league with Edna to patch things up, aren't you?"

Mrs. Knight flushed and turned to Edna, who was studying the ceiling. "Well, Edna did mention something this morning about some difficulties . . ."

Chris shook her finger at Edna. "Your meddling has gone too far this time."

"Bunch of dang silliness," Edna snorted. "Making a ruckus over nothing," she told her niece. "And you!" she turned on Ken. "You don't know beans about what you're doing. You let her slip through your fingers."

There was a noticeable silence in the lobby. The

sounds of hammering and sawing had been replaced with whispers and stifled chuckles. Ken reached behind his mother and closed the office door. "I have to make a phone call about a new heating system. It'll only take a minute, and then I can leave for a while. I'd be delighted to take you two ladies to brunch."

"Nonsense," his mother said. "I came all the way down here to meet Chris. I'd like to see the ice arena, and then we can all go to brunch."

Ken was silent for a moment while he contemplated his options. He sighed and checked his watch. "Okay, but I haven't much time . . ."

Chris scowled at him. Haven't much time? For his mother? Isn't that typical, she fumed. Kenneth Knight, Big Tycoon! Chris linked her arms with the two women. "Come on, I'll give you the grand tour, and then we can find someplace quiet for a cup of tea. We really don't need Ken along, at all."

"Hmmmph," Edna grunted. "Of course we need Ken. How do you expect to plan a wedding without the groom?"

Chris stopped short. "There isn't going to be a wedding."

Edna narrowed her eyes. "That's what you think. I'm no quitter. Ken's the perfect husband for you."

"Yeah," Ken mumbled. "No one else is rich enough to afford the medical insurance."

Chris whirled around and glared at him, nose to nose. "What a horrid thing to say. I've never said a word about your poisonous food, but you bring broken bones into the conversation every chance you get."

He looked genuinely injured. "What do you mean . . . poisonous food?"

"You tried to make me eat a potholder!"

Edna shook her head. "This isn't going too good," she told Margaret Knight.

"Are you sure they used to like each other?"

"Maybe we should just plan the wedding without them," Edna mused.

Ken and Chris exchanged looks of exasperated disbelief. "The heating system can wait," Ken decided. "Let's just get them out of here."

Chris sat with her fingers curled around a cup of cold coffee. The conversation buzzing around her was grimly fascinating. So fascinating that for the second time that morning she forgot to drink her coffee. Edna and Margaret were planning a wedding.

"It should be a Christmas wedding," Edna pronounced. "Christmas weddings are nice."

Margaret agreed. "I had a spring wedding, but if I had it to do again it would definitely be a Christmas wedding. I think it's so nice when you can decorate with holly and red bows."

Chris looked at the man sitting silently beside her. He, too, was absorbed in the older women's conversation. He relaxed against the padded cushion of the booth, his long legs reaching almost to the side occupied by Edna and his mother. One hand held his empty coffee cup, the other unconsciously traced circular patterns across Chris's shoulder and along her neck. A bemused expression hovered at his mouth and lurked in his eyes.

"I think spice cake is good for a December wedding," Margaret said. "Of course it should have white icing and be decorated like any other wedding cake, but if the inside were spice, it would be nice."

Chris wriggled to get Ken's attention. "How can you let them go on like this?" she whispered. "How can you just sit there smiling?"

"They're enjoying themselves. Anyway, I don't know how to stop them."

"Now I know why you got along so well with Aunt Edna."

Ken grinned. "She's just like my mom."

Chris looked at Ken sidewise. "I'm not going to marry you."

"Of course not." The circles at her neck grew lazier, more provocative.

He has great thumbs, Chris thought. *It's the thumbs that make the difference between a good massage and a great massage.* Little prickles of pleasure warmed her skin.

He leaned against her, snuggling her against his chest and his shoulder. "They don't even know we're here."

"Mmmmm," she agreed, her curly lashes drooping over slightly glazed eyes.

"You've got a big family, Margaret," Edna worried. "We wouldn't want to leave anyone out, but I don't know if I can fit such a bunch of people into the town house. I suppose we could hire out a restaurant room."

The two women looked depressed at the thought. "Those restaurant weddings always seem so cold," Margaret finally said.

Edna looked hopeful. "How about your house? Is your house in Pennsylvania big enough to hold everyone?"

"I don't know. It's a nice house, but it's not real big. It's pretty much busting at the seams during holidays."

Chris was startled out of her trance by Ken's deep voice joining the conversation. "How about Darby Hills?"

Chris sat up straight and squeaked, "Are you crazy?"

Ken chuckled and tweaked an orange curl.

"What's Darby Hills?" Edna asked.

Margaret beamed. "It's this huge awful house he bought. It sits on this little hill like a fat lady squatting on an orange."

Edna shivered. "It don't sound like a place for a wedding."

"It's not that bad," Chris offered. "The land around it is really beautiful. There are cows and big oak trees and lots of azaleas . . ." She stopped short and flushed red. She closed her eyes tight and sank into her seat, unable to believe she'd just risen to the defense of Darby Hills. She opened one eye and glared at Ken, daring him to even crack a smile.

Ken's eyes were wide with surprise. Edna and Margaret stared at her openmouthed. Chris grabbed her cup of cold coffee and drained it.

"I'm not going to touch this one," Ken assured Chris. "I don't mind a little danger in my life every now and then, but I'm not suicidal."

Chris looked at her watch. "I should be getting back to the rink."

Ken reached across the table and took his mother's hand. "What are your plans, Mom? How long will you be down here?"

"I'm just here for the day. I drove down with your sister."

"Erin? Where is she?"

Margaret elbowed Edna, and the two women giggled.

"She was chicken," Edna answered with a mischievous grin. "She wouldn't come with us."

Ken's mother smoothed her napkin on the table in front of her. "Erin decided to stay at Edna's town house while we visited with you and Chris, and then this afternoon we're going into Washington together. We're going to be tourists."

The sadness returned to Ken's eyes. "I'd like to take you out to dinner, but I have to get ready to go to Chicago."

"I understand. You take care of yourself. You look so tired."

He did look tired, Chris thought. There were times when the animation returned to his face and his smile reached his eyes, but there were also dark circles and lines of tension that testified to sleepless nights.

He took out a billfold and removed a credit card. "You take this and have a nice afternoon.

Take Erin out to lunch. Someplace fancy." He stood and pulled Chris out of the booth. "We're only a short distance from the rink. I'll walk back with Chris. You can take your time over another cup of coffee here and then drive Edna home in the Mercedes."

Edna turned to Margaret, explaining ruefully, "I don't drive. It's the one thing I don't do. Tried it from time to time but couldn't get the hang of it."

Chris leaned toward Ken and told him in an aside, "Leadfoot smashed up every car she ever tried to drive. One time in Denver she put Uncle Ed's station wagon into reverse and took out the garage door."

"I heard that!" Edna snapped. "That wasn't my fault. It was that dang electronic door opener that didn't work right. Besides, my foot slipped. I didn't mean to go just then."

Ken trundled Chris into her ski jacket and pushed her toward the door. "Don't you know that discretion is the better part of valor? Edna will feed you lima bean soup tonight for that crack about her driving."

"I hate lima bean soup."

"I know," he said softly.

Chris felt a lump form in her throat at the tender intimacy of his response. They stopped and looked into each other's eyes for a long moment. Chris saw questions there—questions that had no answers. And regret. She knew her eyes reflected the same. Tears prickled deep inside her. She felt them spill over her lower lashes and slide down her cheeks.

Ken stared silently at the tears for a moment. He pressed his lips together and brushed his thumb gently across her cheeks. "I wish I could make you happy," he said, his voice hoarse with emotion. He gathered her to his chest and held her close, bowing his head into her hair and closing his eyes against its softness. "I know you're scared and angry, and I obviously did a lot of things wrong. But now I don't know how to make them right." He pressed a lingering kiss against her ear.

She trembled against him, not knowing what to say. This morning he hadn't seemed to care at all, and now he seemed to love her again. Maybe he was just a sucker for tears, she thought. Or maybe sitting together in the booth had triggered a testosterone attack. Although, there were none of the obvious signs . . .

A horn blared at them, and a truck pulled into the restaurant parking lot. A burly young man leaned out of the truck window. "We've got problems," he called to Ken. "The new compressor was just delivered, and Marty says it's not the right one."

"Of course," Ken muttered. "Murphy's Law. If anything can go wrong . . . it will." He wrapped an arm around Chris. "Come on, we'll hitch a ride back with Steve."

Chris quickly wiped away the last remnants of tears and slid up onto the large bench seat of the Ford. Ken read her mind as he took his place next to her. "Yeah"—he smiled regretfully—"life would be a lot less complicated if my truck had been this big."

Paint cans and carpenters' paraphernalia had been stacked in the corner of the box office. A spattered tan dropcloth covered tables and chairs. A bare forty-watt bulb hung from the ceiling, shedding a depressing circle of grim light on the papers in front of Chris. She stared blank-faced at her surroundings, feeling as if she'd been pushed into a corner, both literally and figuratively. A mound of paperwork and the prospect of coming eyeball to eyeball with Ken had kept her chained to her desk. For a fleeting moment in the restaurant parking lot, Chris had thought she felt something holding them together . . . a gossamer-thin, fragile thread of caring and affection. And then it was gone. Broken by the honking of a truck horn.

So here I sit, she brooded. *Hiding in here like a stupid fugitive.* She rested her chin on her hand. It was damn depressing: She loved a man who didn't exist; her aunt was planning a wedding that would never take place; and she worked for a skating rink that, as far as she could tell, didn't have a name.

Ken stood in the open doorway and watched her. Finally, he forced his mouth into a tight smile. "I'll bet my problems are worse than yours."

Chris looked up and stared at him stonily.

He slouched against the door and tucked his hands into his pockets. "The compressor is all wrong," he offered.

"Who cares?"

"You should care. We can't make ice without a compressor."

I don't want to make ice, she thought miserably. *I want to make love.*

He turned away from her and poured himself half a cup of coffee. He drank it in silence and threw the paper cup into the trash. "I'd like to oversee this project personally, but I can't. It's going to be up to you and Marty to make sure the rink opens in a week." He took a business card from his wallet and scribbled a number on it. "This is where I can be reached in Chicago. If there are any problems, business or otherwise, give me a call."

Chris' hand clenched, inadvertently crumpling the card, as she made a mental note never again to fall in love. "And what consitutes an 'otherwise' problem? Canceling the caterer and the florist? You could afford to sit in that damn restaurant and chuckle about all of this. You're flying off to Chicago. And who knows where you'll spend the week after that . . . Bangkok? Zanzibar? I have to stay here and live with Edna. I have to somehow convince her that there will not be a wedding taking place."

Ken looked at her levelly for a full minute. His mouth quirked into a smile that Chris thought looked slightly fiendish. "Do you think she'd actually go ahead and plan a wedding?"

Chris threw her hands into the air. "Of course, she'd go ahead and plan a wedding. You don't know what it's like to stop her once she sets her mind on something." Chris sank back into her chair. "Maybe I should just let her go ahead and plan the wedding and book myself on a flight to Orlando the night before."

"There's another alternative." Ken grinned wolfishly. "We could go ahead and get married.

I could probably fit it into my schedule if I leave Zanzibar out of my itinerary."

Without thinking, Chris grabbed the electric pencil sharpener and hurled it at him. It whistled past his ear and smashed against the door. Ken looked unperturbed. The infuriating smile stayed on his lips. "I suppose that means I can go to Zanzibar, after all." He picked up the undamaged sharpener and placed it on a paint can well out of Chris' reach. "I've made arrangements for Steve to take you home. He'll be here until five. Just look him up when you want to leave."

"You're going now?"

"Do you care?"

"No!"

"Hmmmm." He smiled pleasantly, slipped out of the office, and closed the door behind him.

Chris stared at the door for a long time before she realized she was smiling, too. "Damn!"

Chapter 12

Chris stood at curbside, looking balefully at her new car. It was a glistening black Mustang with a black spoiler, and custom striping. And it was a mistake. A twenty-thousand-dollar mistake with black leather upholstery and a sound system that could shatter glass. "You're a great car," she told it, "but you were destined for somebody else." Chris paced on the sidewalk. She'd wanted to get a little front-wheel drive station wagon—something sensible. Something cheap. She sighed. She didn't know what had come over her in the car lot. Suddenly, she'd had this craving for power and flash— and the day before she'd slunk into a naughty lingerie store and bought a black lace garter belt. Chris made a questioning gesture at the car. "Why? Why am I doing these things?" *Because I'm crazy. Kenneth Callahan Knight has made me crazy. Look at this. He has me talking to cars.*

She looked over at the Mercedes, also parked at

curbside. Tasteful, she thought. Understated elegance. Not the sort of car a woman who owns a black lace garter belt would drive. It has to go back to Darby Hills; there's no reason to keep it. Chris sighed and ran her hand along a sleek silver fender. The truth was, she admitted reluctantly, she hated to see it go: *I miss Ken more than I ever thought possible, and I like driving his car.* The car had become a tenuous thread that bound her to him; when she returned the car, one more tie would be severed.

It had been two weeks since Ken had left for Chicago. Somehow he'd managed to send her postcards from around the world. Bangkok. Singapore. Zurich. Lima.

"Dear Chris," he'd written on the Bangkok card. "Business is taking longer than expected and Bangkok is lonely without you." The last card she'd received had been mailed from Calcutta. "Business is finally done here in Calcutta. Next stop on my itinerary is Zanzibar. I hear they're expecting an epidemic of bubonic plague and typhoid. Do you think I should cancel?"

Why was it so hard to say yes? Chris groaned. Why couldn't she just tell him to cancel Zanzibar and come home and marry her. Why couldn't she admit, "You're right, Ken Callahan Knight . . . I fabricated a bad guy because I was afraid to make a commitment." Chris wasn't sure. She still felt doubt and uneasiness. There was something about him that disturbed her—something skulking around in the dark corners of her mind. Chris thought of the beautiful diamond ring, another symbol of her inability to make a decision; it wasn't on her finger, and it wasn't in his pocket. It was in never-never land. Ignominiously relegated to life in a cup by the toaster. Yuk, she thought, turning from the Mercedes and heading for her front door, what an indecisive wimp. She was a disgrace to her new black Mustang and her wicked lace garter belt.

Lucy flung the door open and threw herself into her mother's arms. "I got a A on my spelling test, and we got flowers! A man came and delivered them. And Aunt Edna wouldn't let me open the card. She said we had to wait for you."

Chris looked at Edna. "Flowers?"

Edna took the small yellow envelope from the kitchen counter and handed it to Chris.

Chris struggled with the sealed envelope. She held the note card in front of her and read out loud. "Arrived Darby Hills. Need instructions regarding Zanzibar." Chris smiled. "Ken's home."

"Seems like a funny note. I don't understand any of it. What's this business about Zanzibar?"

"Inside joke." Chris snitched a cucumber slice from the salad bowl. "Let's eat. I'm famished."

It was a no-pressure message, Chris decided later that night. Ken could have called when he got home, but that would have required an immediate response from her. The note gave her time. It gave her a chance to come to terms with her feelings and plot a course of action. She thought of the quiet smile that had been on his face when he'd left. She'd thought about that smile a lot. It was not the smile of a man who was angry, or mad, or heartbroken, and it certainly wasn't the smile of a man who had lost interest. It was the smile of a man who thought he might eventually win. It was patient and gentle with love. Chris wrinkled her nose. Very different from the cold shoulder he'd given her in Boston when he'd returned her key.

Chris took the key ring from the hook on the bulletin board. She held it in her hand and remembered how she'd felt that morning when he'd moved into her life. Obviously, the key hadn't been as significant to him as it had been to her. She could never have parted with it as easily as he had. She looked at the key in the dim light of the silent kitchen, glad that Edna and Lucy had gone to bed early. If she was going to get maudlin over a stupid key, she'd rather do it in private.

It was the first time she'd really looked at the key since he'd returned it to her. Suddenly, her eyes opened wide and a smile creased her face. "That sneak!" Chris ran to her purse and got her key chain, then put the two house keys on the table and compared them. They were different. He hadn't returned the key to her house, he'd given her the key to *his* house! She held it up to the light and examined it more closely. DARBY HILLS had been inscribed on it in tiny letters.

Chris felt as if her heart would burst. Kenneth Knight had given her that key. She knew it was Knight because he'd been clean-shaven and immaculately groomed. And it had been Knight who'd recognized her tears of frustration and confusion in the restaurant parking lot, and who'd held her close, wanting to erase the pain. She cocked an eyebrow. Of course, it also had been Knight who'd gone off on business trips and never even called to say hello. Big deal, she told herself, that's hardly a criminal offense.

She felt obligated to enumerate another fault: It had been Knight who'd bought the rink on the sly.

Chris sank lower in her chair. He'd bought the rink and turned it into a first-rate training center, making her wildest dreams come true—not exactly something you could give him a black mark for. She sought out the real reason for her discomfort. What was it about him that scared her so? And then, finally, she realized that it was the whole man.

Combined, the personalities of Ken Callahan and Kenneth Knight created an overwhelming, complicated mixture of masculinity that she knew she could never totally understand and certainly could never control. And if she couldn't do either of those things, how could she keep him? She would lose him just as she'd lost her first husband. Chris wrinkled her nose. Was that really what she'd been worried about? It sounded dumb. It was like never eating peas because you hated brussels sprouts. Just because they were both green and round didn't make them identical. At the ripe old age of twenty-nine she might be incredibly inexperienced in the mating game, but she should have known the real thing when it came along, she scolded herself.

She had consistently underestimated Ken. And she'd underestimated the depth and scope of their love. He would never leave her . . . and it was impossible for her to leave him. The revelation didn't hit like a thunderbolt. It was more like molten molasses that crept along brainy crevices, soothing, healing, filling corridors of despair and doubt with hope and courage and joyous security. She held the key in the palm of her hand. It was the key that had opened the door to enlightenment. The key. The smile. And Zanzibar. He had hung in there. There had been times when he'd been angry, but he'd never deserted her . . . not even when she'd kicked him out of her house.

Chris looked at the clock on the wall. Nine o'clock. She could be at Darby Hills by ten. She gave herself a mental hug and slipped Ken's key onto her key chain. She snatched her ski jacket from the hall closet and closed the front door quietly behind her. Chris was halfway down the sidewalk when she remembered the ring. She thunked her head and went back inside. How could she possibly go anywhere without her ring? She was practically naked without it! She looked down at the diamond sparkling reproachfully in the cup and apologized. "Sorry," she whispered, "I've been a real cluck." She slipped the ring onto her finger and thought for a moment just how right it felt. Locking the door behind her once again, she took a moment to enjoy the cold air that prickled on her flushed cheeks and to wonder at the beauty of the sliver of golden moon that hung low in the navy night sky.

Chris considered the two cars at her disposal for a moment, then chose the Mercedes, making a mental note to enroll Edna in driving school first thing in the morning. The Mustang would fit her perfectly. Chris doubled over with laughter at the idea of little Aunt Edna terrorizing the neighborhood in the flashy black car. And she'd be a celebrity at her next senior citizens meeting!

When her laughter had subsided, Chris was plagued with more somber thoughts. *What on Earth can I say to Ken?* she worried. *I've been such a boob.* She turned onto Little River Turnpike and headed west toward Middleburg, winding her way through Fairfax City. Traffic thinned dramatically once she reached the county line, and she relaxed and enjoyed the solitude. A few stars blinked on. She approached Middleburg and was reminded that it was the Christmas season as she drove past candles burning in small-paned windows framed by ruffled white colonial curtains. Green wreaths and red bows adorned doors. Holly garlands wrapped around front-yard gaslights. Chris hummed a few bars of "Deck the Halls" and wondered about

Darby Hills. Surely, it was not as awful as she remembered it . . . and she'd never gone inside. The inside was probably very nice.

Chris drove on out of town and searched for the road leading to Ken's estate, wishing she'd been more attentive on her previous visit. Crossing her fingers for luck, she turned at the next intersection, following instinct more than memory. After a mile she suspected she was on the right route. The private drive appeared to her right. She turned and gave a sigh of relief when her headlights bounced off the gold plaque. She reached into the glove compartment and found the controls to open the gate, and for the first time since she'd discovered the secret of the key, Chris felt the familiar butterflies of fear fluttering in her stomach. The narrow drive stretching in front of her looked ominously black. The steers that by daylight looked so placid and picturesque had turned into brooding bovine hulks.

Courage, she admonished herself, *don't let your imagination run wild.* She passed the caretaker's house and was relieved to see it decorated for Christmas in traditional Middleburg style. Light shone from every window, giving the impression that this was a home filled with activity, but the cheery scene didn't ease her nervousness. She was pleased to replace the image of Vincent Price with Paddy O'Grady as caretaker, but the feeling of trespass remained. She approached the thicket of trees separating the main house from the servants' area and scolded herself for not calling first. Taking a deep breath, she encouraged the Mercedes to roll along the winding road. The trees thinned, and Chris found herself gaping in chilled horror at the sight in front of her.

The mansion sat on the dwarfed hillock like a huge black lump. It was more menacing, more forbidding, and twice as ugly as she'd remembered it. Not a single light shone out in welcome. Chris gripped the wheel and eased the car forward. A rude four-letter word escaped from her tight throat. Thinking of Aunt Edna she quickly amended the phrase to "Oh, sugar," but it seemed a little mild in view of the monstrosity looming in front of her. She decided there were three possibilities: No one was home, everyone was asleep, or this was all a bad dream. She wiped her sweaty palms on her jeans and nudged the car onward. It was no big deal. She'd simply go on home and call him in the morning. She'd whip right around the big circular drive and get her fanny the heck out of here. No one would ever know. Not Vincent Price or Paddy O'Grady. Only the big stupid cows would know, and they looked like they could keep a secret.

She was well past the front entrance when she realized she'd passed Ken's truck. Chris stopped and looked in her rearview mirror. Yes, it was definitely his truck. And it was parked at a rakish angle to the front entrance, leaving no doubt in her mind that he'd zoomed up to the house, screeched to a stop, and run inside. She chewed her lip, threw her hands into the air, and shifted into reverse. What the heck!

At the front door, Chris stiffened her back and searched for a doorbell, but she couldn't find one in the darkness. She rapped on the massive block of carved wood and waited. Nothing. She put her ear to the door and listened. Silence. "Well," she said out loud to bolster her spirits, "good thing I have a key." She cracked her knuckles and looked around. Now or never, she told herself. Anyway, what was the big deal? He'd given her a key to his house, and this was his house. So, why shouldn't she use the key? Holding her breath, she closed her eyes and plunged the key into the big gold lock. The ornate door swung open easily, revealing a foyer large enough to accommodate a soccer match. Chris took a cursory glance at polished wood banisters and massive oil paintings and focused her attention on a ray of light sliding under a doorjamb toward the back of the house. A shiver ran down her spine as she walked across the marble floor. It was like being in a deserted hotel. It was hard to believe anyone actually lived here. Especially Ken. Ken who colored Pilgrims orange and purple, and who loved cookies and baked macaroni.

Chris followed the light and stopped just outside the half-open door. The sounds of a crackling fire and television drifted out to her. She peeked inside and saw that this was a library. The walls were lined with leather-bound volumes, the floors were covered with oriental rugs, and the furniture consisted of massive manly leather chairs and an enormous leather-topped, chairman-of-the-board-type desk. The room was dominated by a stone fireplace that stretched across half a wall. Chris recognized a familiar form hunched in front of the fire and raised a hand to her mouth in relief and astonishment. Ken and Bob the dog were roasting hot dogs and watching TV.

"What on earth are you doing?" Chris grinned.

Ken turned and stood. One hand dangled at his side. The other held a long fork with a black hot dog speared on the end. He wore jeans and a faded T-shirt. His ebony hair was backlighted by the fire. It was in need of a cut again, falling in waves over his ears, and Chris felt her heart flip as a broad smile flashed white in his permanently tanned face. "I'm cooking supper."

Chris looked at the small television set on the floor. "And watching TV?"

"Just for the noise. I hate this house. It's like living in a mausoleum."

"Where is everybody? Aren't there servants?"

"A whole pack of them. A butler, a cook, a chauffeur, and God knows how many maids."

Chris raised her eyebrows.

"I know what you're thinking, but these maids are *old*. I inherited them with the house, and there's not a single one that doesn't need support hose."

"So where are they?"

Ken tested his hot dog with his finger to see if it was hot. "My estate supervisor is having a crew come in to paint this barn and thought it would be easier if he didn't have to deal with my decrepit household staff, so we sent the old folks off for a week."

Chris regarded the lone frankfurter. "This looks like fun, but couldn't you construct a more nourishing meal in the kitchen?"

"My cook would kill me if I got anything out of place. And besides, the kitchen scares the hell out of me. It's all stainless steel—cabinets, appliances, and pots and pans. It reminds me of the embalming room in a morgue. The only thing missing is a tilt-top table."

Chris smiled and knelt in front of the fire. "This library's nice."

"It's my favorite room." He put the hot dog on a plate on the hearth and gestured to a large window opposite the desk. "That window opens on the back of the house. I can sit here and watch the cows."

Chris looked at him in wonderment. Kenneth Knight . . . watching cows?

He grinned at her. "I like cows."

Chris burst out laughing. "You like everything."

He sat beside her on the rug. He reached out and twirled a strand of her hair, causing goose bumps to erupt over ninety percent of her body. "I like you."

Chris turned her eyes to the fire while she tried to catch her breath. She felt his hand trail along the line of her jaw and drop to the zipper on her jacket.

He slid the zipper down and parted her jacket,

revealing a soft yellow cotton sweater. When he finally raised his eyes to hers, they were black with passion. "I see you're wearing my ring."

"Mmmmm." Chris smiled, discarding her jacket. "I had to use the cup for hot chocolate and didn't have any place else to put the ring." She leaned forward and ran her hands under his shirt, smoothing them across his tight stomach. "Why are you having the house painted? Planning on having a party? Or a wedding reception, maybe?"

Ken blinked. "The house painted?" He closed his eyes and tried to concentrate. "Honey, if you want me to answer questions, you're going to have to stop touching me!"

Chris drew away from him. "I do have a few questions . . ."

"Mmmm."

"Do you still want to marry me?"

His eyes held hers in solemn adoration. "Yes."

Chris felt tears trickle down the back of her throat. She loved him so desperately, but she had to ask. "About your work, will a family interfere? All that traveling that you do . . ."

"All that traveling has ended. I've spent the last six months consolidating and selling and transferring power to good people. I'm not chairman-of-the-board material. I like being in jeans and sweatshirts and taking my dog to work with me." He stirred the logs in the fireplace. "I'm not nearly as rich as I've been made out to be, but I'm very comfortable."

"Comfortable enough to afford a skating rink as a 'toy'?"

"Yes. But I don't really consider it a toy. I think what you're doing is important. I want Patti to have her chance. I like the idea of helping young athletes." He grinned his little-boy grin at her. "I've hired myself as rink manager—not only will we be able to work together, but I'll get to run the Zamboni!"

Chris smiled at the thought of Ken atop the Zamboni. "I love you."

"Does that mean I should cancel Zanzibar?"

Chris lowered her eyes and heard a sound emerge from deep in her throat. Something between a purr and a growl. She unbuttoned his shirt.

Ken fell back onto the rug and pulled Chris on top of him. "Okay, vixen," he growled, smiling huskily, "what other sweet tortures are you going to inflict on me?"

Chris looked at him in mock innocence. "I don't know what you mean by sweet tortures."

He rolled her over and straddled her. His eyes

were soft and molten, heavy lidded with hungry passion. "Sweet tortures," he repeated. "Like this." He leaned forward and kissed her parted lips, allowing her to sample only a small portion of the passion he held for her. "I've had two long weeks of sleepless nights to think of sweet tortures," he whispered. "It will take me a lifetime to show them all to you."

The Rocky Road to Romance

Her tall, dark, and deliciously dangerous boss . . .

When the delightful, daffy Dog Lady of station WZZZ offered to take on the temporary job of traffic reporter, Steve Crow tried to think of reasons to turn Daisy Adams down. Perhaps he knew that sharing the close quarters of a car with her for hours would give the handsome program director no room to resist her quirky charms. He'd always favored low-slung sports cars and high-heeled women, but that was before he fell for a free spirit who caught crooks by accident, loved old people and pets, and had just too many jobs!

Loving Daisy turned Steve's life upside down, especially once he adopted Bob, a huge dog masquerading as a couch potato. But was Daisy finally ready to play for keeps?

Love Overboard

Sinfully handsome schooner captain Ivan Rasmussen deserved to be called Ivan the Terrible, Stephanie Lowe decided. First he'd sold her a haunted house, and now he was laughing at her Calamity Jane cooking! She'd only agreed to work one voyage of his Maine coastal cruise in exchange for the house repairs promised by her cousin, who'd run off to marry a plumber.

But the brazen Ivan, descendant of a pirate, insisted on flirting with her. When the voyage ended, he even managed to be on hand to help her trap the "ghost" in her house. Fun and comic mayhem, as only Janet Evanovich can write it.

Back to the Bedroom

For months he'd thought of her as the Mystery Woman, draped in black velvet cloak, with outrageous red curls, flawless skin, and carrying a large, odd case. But the night David Dodd sees a helicopter drop a chunk of metal through the roof of his lovely neighbor's bedroom, he gets to meet the formidable and delightful Katherine Finn at last!

Kate is a driven concert musician with more commitments than hours in the day. Dave is a likable slacker who seems to be drifting through life. Yet, no one has ever made her feel as cherished, and she's never had so much fun, even though her eccentric boarder, Elise, assures her that where Kate is concerned, Dave has plenty of ambition.

Manhunt

Alexandra Scott, Alaskan Wilderness Woman. It had a terrific ring to it, but Alex felt a sudden twinge of uncertainty. She'd traded in her Wall Street job and fancy condo for a rundown cabin in the woods and a bait & tackle store. She'd wanted to escape the rat race and to go husband-hunting where men outnumbered women four to one, but was she ready for the challenge?

Then she spotted Michael Casey, a sexy pilot who was undaunted by disaster, had hero written all over him . . . and was a confirmed bachelor. Michael Casey was the man she had come to Alaska to hunt, and Alexandra Scott had him in her sights.

Smitten

Single mom Lizabeth Kane wasn't exactly construction-worker material, but she truly wanted a job—and Matt Hallahan found her radiant smile utterly irresistible. When he agreed to hire her as a laborer, Lizabeth sent up a cheer. Since her divorce from a snobby philanderer, she'd frankly lost interest in men, but this macho carpenter, who smelled of sawdust and musk, made her senses sizzle.

As for Matt, he was charmed by Lizabeth's enthusiasm, her spunky kids, and wacky aunt. Clearly, this was a match made in heaven.

Thanksgiving

When Megan Murphy discovers a floppy-eared rabbit gnawing on the hem of her skirt, she means to give its careless owner a piece of her mind—but Dr. Patrick Hunter is too attractive to stay mad at for long.

As for Patrick, he wants to play house together and make Thanksgiving dinner for their families. But Megan has wept over one failed love and is afraid to risk her heart again.

Wife for Hire

Hank Mallone spotted trouble when she sat down and said she'd marry him. Maggie Toone was a tempting firecracker who'd make his life delightful hell if he let her pretend to be his wife in order to improve his rogue's reputation. Would his harebrained scheme to get a bank loan for his business backfire once Maggie arrived in his small Vermont town and let the gossips take a look?

Maggie never expected her employer to be drop-dead handsome, or to affect her like a belt of bourbon on an empty stomach, but she was too intrigued by his offer to say no . . . and too eager to escape a life that made her feel trapped. The deal was strictly business, both agreed, until Hank turned out to be every fantasy she'd ever had.

Naughty Neighbor

Louisa Brannigan's neighbor was driving her crazy. He snatched her newspaper and listened through her town house walls. But when she got fired from her government job, Pete was there, asking her to join his undercover operation. So Louisa was hopelessly entangled—professionally speaking—with the sexiest man alive. Sneaking around corners was fun, especially when the getaway car was a Porsche. Suddenly, Louisa was enjoying life on the edge.

Foul Play

When Amy Klasse loses her TV job to a dancing chicken, handsome veterinarian Jake Elliott rescues her with an offer to be his receptionist. Jake just can't resist a damsel in distress, and Amy certainly doesn't mind Jake's charming sincerity.

Then, suddenly, the job-stealing chicken disappears and Amy is suspected of foul play. Amy and Jake search for clues to prove her innocence. But will Jake be able to prove to Amy that love, too, is a mystery worth solving?

The Grand Finale

Berry Knudsen had a talent for disaster, but when she climbed a tree to rescue a kitten, she wasn't prepared for the scrumptious hunk undressing in a nearby window, or her dive downward that smashed Jake Sawyer's pizza and won his heart! But was there room in her chaotic schedule for a risk-taking inventor with dreams?

Berry took classes, delivered pizzas, and cared for three eccentric old ladies she rescued from the train station. But Jake thrived on a challenge, and he could be very inventive. Could he teach her there was time to make butterscotch pudding and let herself be loved?

Hero at Large

It seems like good luck when gorgeous and mysterious Ken Callahan stops to help single mom Chris Nelson with her car. But then she breaks his arm . . . then his toe . . . and then his heart. Not easily discouraged, Ken moves into her basement . . . cooks her potholder in the spaghetti sauce . . . attempts to seduce her with cookies . . . and destroys her favorite pan by trying to make a roast in it. All may seem lost for Chris and Ken, until a meddlesome Aunt Edna, a ride on a Zamboni, and a genuine love of family all conspire to turn their luck around.